The
Dragon
and
her
Boy

PENNY CHRIMES

The Dragon and her Boy

Illustrated by
Levente Szabo

Orion

ORION CHILDREN'S BOOKS

First published in Great Britain in 2021
by Hodder and Stoughton

1 3 5 7 9 10 8 6 4 2

Text copyright © Penny Chrimes, 2021
Illustrations © Levente Szabo, 2021

The moral rights of the author and illustrator have been asserted.

A CIP catalogue record for this book
is available from the British Library.

ISBN 978 1 51010 712 0

Typeset by Hewer Text UK Ltd, Edinburgh
Printed and bound in Great Britain by Clays Ltd, Elcograf S.p.A.

The paper and board used in this book are made
from wood from responsible sources.

Orion Children's Books
An imprint of
Hachette Children's Group
Part of Hodder and Stoughton
Carmelite House
50 Victoria Embankment
London EC4Y 0DZ

An Hachette UK Company

www.hachette.co.uk
www.hachettechildrens.co.uk

For Felix

And to Joshua, Henry,

Emily and Thea.

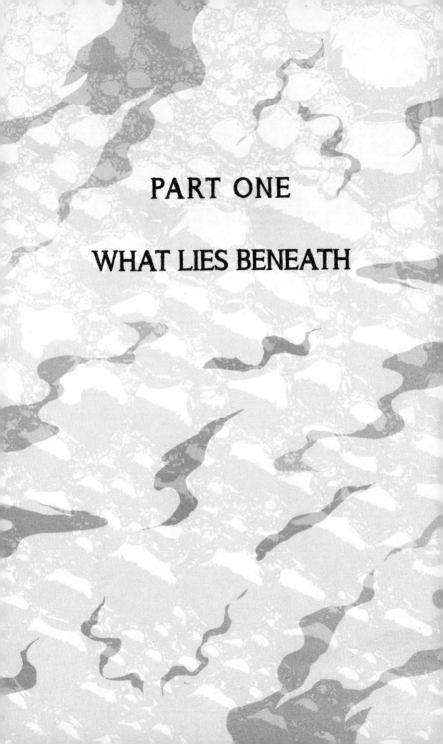

PART ONE

WHAT LIES BENEATH

CHAPTER 1

It was the summer of the Great Heat. And the word on the street was that London was being roasted alive for its sins.

Bartholomew Fair was as hot as a baker's oven that August, and the heat was coming at the tumblers, Stick and Spud and Sparrow, from all sides. The sun had been beating down from above for weeks, but here in the heart of the city there was an uneasy feeling that the heat was now rising from below as well. The tumblers' hands and bare feet were singeing from turning somersaults on the burning cobbles.

"Tain't right, 'tain't normal!' The holiday crowds were all over sweat and full of grumble. 'Old Scratch is blowing on his coals, down there,' they grizzled, keeping a sharp eye on the ground like it might open up any moment beneath

3

their feet. 'And we'll be baked to death in our beds before Bartlemy Fair's over.'

That's what they said, but Stick didn't hold with no Devil. He was a practical lad who dealt only in facts, and he'd never seen Beelzebub or Old Scratch or Old Nick or Old Bendy – or whatever they called it. He didn't need to believe in all that, because he'd got memories buried deep of worse. But that was a long time ago, and he'd never told nobody nowt about any of it. Stick had always been the quiet one, never one to waste words when there was no call for them. Not even with his oldest friend, Fly the chimney-sweep, who had sailed off months before in the company of a tiger, to nobody knew where.

'We've got enough devils to deal with up here,' he remarked to Spud and Sparrow now. 'Without worriting ourselves about what some old varmint that don't even exist is doing down there.'

No, Stick wasn't one to believe in summat he'd never clapped eyes on. But that was before everything happened. Afterwards he wasn't so certain sure what he believed. About anything.

Today there had been no pleasing the overheated and uneasy crowd who normally rained pennies on the tumblers on this, St Bartholomew's Day, the biggest holiday of the

4

year. Earlier that morning, the boys had promised to treat the other gutterlings – their gang of fellow street urchins – to a pennyworth of pudding apiece when they met up again that night. But right now it didn't look like they'd even make enough to fill their own bellies.

In the end, Stick and Spud and Sparrow had given up chucking cartenwheels from blistered hands to blistered feet and back again for no thanks, and were taking a break for a while the right way up. An ominous heat-haze brooded over Smithfield, thick with the stink of evaporating blood from the meat market. The tumblers' palms were red from the stained cobbles.

Skinny as a row of skittles, the three of them barely had a full set of togs between them. None of their tattered rags met in the middle, but on a day like this, for once it was no bad thing to have a few gaps to let the air in.

Stick, the thinker – acknowledged by all the gutterlings to be the best at plans and wheezes since Fly had gone – was as long and thin as a pencil. His face was long and thin to match, with hair and brows as black as boot polish, beneath which his grey eyes twinkled, bright as brimstone. He was almost too tall now for tumbling, though it meant that his legs were long enough to tie up in knots like a German sausage, which always made the toffs laugh.

5

Spud was the stubborn one, especially when it came to getting ha'pennies out of the customers. He was a little rounder, and his face was pockmarked like a potato from a near-death brush with the smallpox, which is how he'd earned his nickname. He wasn't as naturally nimble as the other two, but he'd taught himself to roll head over heels as neat and quick as a woodlouse.

Spud had always been a straight-talker – he'd had to stop working as a crossing-sweeper, because he'd given offence to so many toffs who'd walked across his nicely swept crossing and not tipped him so much as a farthing. Even now he was a tumbler, he wasn't one for flummery when the customers didn't come up with the tips.

'Fungus-faced old fossils!' Spud yelled now after an elderly couple who had watched the whole show but sidled off without a tip. 'Fair's fair,' he added. ''Tain't right.' Such penny-pinching offended Spud's strongly held sense of right and wrong.

'What the mischief's up with them all today?' he grumbled. 'Sour-faced skinflints!'

He made sure he was speaking loud enough to give offence. Spud prided himself on a fine repertoire of foul-mouthed insults, which was at odds with his choir-boy smile. Together with his mop of curls, which might have been fair if he'd ever washed, his smile gave him the air of a smut-stained cherub who had somehow tumbled out of heaven and got lost in the gutter.

Last and very much least came Sparrow. He'd been bought from the workhouse by a house-breaker almost as soon as he could walk, because he was so tiny he could be shoved through even the smallest window, and then sneak round to open the front door. But the work hadn't suited Sparrow, who didn't see why he should risk hanging just to steal stuff for other people. First chance he'd got, he ran away to join the gutterlings on the streets, and turned his skills to tumbling instead.

Sparrow was the smallest of the three, but he was also the sharpest at spotting food and danger. He never seemed to grow, no matter how much food he managed to snabble. He was no more than a basket of bird-bones with rags for feathers, and his clothes were the most threadbare because the reach-me-downs always came to him last. He was so skinny and light he could chuck a dozen handsprings in a row, and got extra tips for tumbling on tables without touching a single glass.

'Here – look what I has prigged . . .' Sparrow plunged under the nearby stalls and came back clutching a paper twist full of fried fish that had been left unguarded.

Spud seized a grubby fistful. 'Cor, me belly thought me throat'd been cut!' It was the first time the tumblers had eaten and it was full on midday, by the height of the sun.

Stick leaned back against a wall after he'd taken his share, the soot-stained brick burning through his threadbare shirt, and surveyed the packed fairground crowd that was heaving like the surface of the sea before a storm. Spud and Sparrow were still heads-down, licking the last grains of salt from the fish paper. He took out his never-lit pipe and clenched it between his teeth, one knee bent and one bare foot propping up the wall. Anyone who knew Stick would know Stick was thinking.

'Something ain't right,' he observed, to no one in particular.

The air shifted and sighed, so thick you could have sliced it with a bread knife and toasted it with dripping.

'Show! Show! Show! Show!' The panting, sweating crowd had gathered around a tall red-and-white-striped puppet booth, where Punch was loading his wife Judy into a wheelbarrow and was trundling her towards the mouth of a dragon, urged on by hysterical gin-soaked onlookers.

'That's the way to do it, Mr Punch!' They pressed against the rickety tent, baying for Mrs Punch's blood, until it swayed and almost pitched over. 'Feed her to the beast!'

Their shouts mingled with Punch's cackles and Judy's

8

screams and the roar of the dragon. Above it all echoed the cries of a preacher, all trussed up in black with a face like a dying duck in a thunderstorm and intent on spoiling everyone's fun.

'Repent,' the preacher was shouting, 'for the Day of Judgement is upon you!'

Then several things happened at once and nothing was ever the same after that.

A suffocating blast of hot air blew up from below, enveloping the fairground, blowing the women's skirts up like balloons and scorching the hairs on the men's shins. It felt like it came from a pair of great bellows deep underground. It sounded like a sigh, a groan of immense weariness, and it smelled of bad eggs and something long-buried.

There was a lot of screaming and a dozen women went down in a faint. The surface of the earth rippled gently, like a snake getting ready to shuffle off its skin.

The crowd, which a moment before had been shrieking for Mrs Punch's blood, fell silent. It wasn't a normal state of affairs to feel the earth moving beneath your feet, even after so many hours of jollification. The most rickety of the stalls swayed and buckled, sending trinkets and treats and jiggumbobs spilling out on to the cobbles.

9

Stick propped himself more securely against his wall and waited for what would come next. He clenched his teeth on his pipe to steady his nerves. All was still for a moment, but he somehow knew in his long bones that this was just the start.

Out of the silence, the whispers started up.

'That preacher were right, 'tis the Day of Judgement . . .'

'Old Nick is on his way . . .'

'And me not even washed me smalls!'

Then the earth bucked violently and gave a mighty heave, like the innards of a pie, hot from the oven, bubbling up to shake off its crust.

Bartlemy's two church towers lurched like a pair of drunks too tossicated to stand upright, and congealed blood from the meat market melted and bubbled up between the loosened cobbles.

'Saints alive!'

'What in thunderation . . .?'

'S'help me! 'Tis the end of days . . .'

The puppet booth collapsed in a heap. The shrieking crowd went down like ninepins, and the tumblers went down with them – all but Stick, with the wall still propping up his back.

So Stick was the only one standing a few minutes later when a lone man emerged from the chaos and comflobstigation. The man was strikingly tall, with a chimney-pipe hat so high you couldn't see where it stopped and the sky started.

Cor, Stick thought. *You could keep a meat pudding hot in that hat!*

Beneath the hat, the man's nose stuck out, sharp as a pickaxe, from a beetroot-red face laced with bulging blue veins. His jacket flapped open to reveal a richly embroidered waistcoat of the same purple as his cheeks. It was straining at the buttons, over a great beer-barrel of a chest.

Stick couldn't take his eyes off him. Something was trying to crawl out of the cupboard in the back of Stick's head, where he'd locked up all the bad stuff.

'He's dressed like a toff,' he muttered uneasily. 'But he's built like a brickie.'

Over one shoulder the man was carrying a large sack that was bulging and wriggling like it was full of live eels, and he held a tightly rolled umbrella, which he was brandishing like a weapon. He was swearing at the drunks who were too comfoozled to get out of the way. 'You fools . . . you know not what lies beneath!'

Why's that cove need an umbyrelly on a day like this? thought Stick. It was an odd thought to bother his head

11

with, when the world was in the process of turning upside down, but it seemed somehow important.

Confused noises were coming from the bag, and the man gave it a few hard blows with the umbrella until the noises stopped. 'Cut your clack,' he growled. 'You'll be fresh meat soon enough.'

At that moment, the man turned his face full towards Stick. His burning eyes were full of savagery and greed – he had the look of a man possessed. But it wasn't just the madness in those eyes that made Stick turn quickly away and duck his head.

'It can't be him . . . not here . . . not him . . .' Stick's voice was shaking, but nobody was close, so nobody heard the fear. 'I thought he were dead . . . leastwise, I hoped he were.'

By the time Stick cautiously looked up again, the man had gone, as suddenly as he had appeared, and all around the fairground the rattled and befuddled crowd were struggling back to their feet.

'Blimey, what a to-do!'

'Bust me! What do they put in that beer?'

'Never known nowt like it in all my born days!'

'Ought to be a law against it!'

Soon the fainting women were fanned and set back on their feet, and the usual clamjamfry of Bartlemy Fair was restored. It wasn't long before the holiday crowd had forgotten the moment the earth moved beneath their feet.

But Mr Punch and his long-suffering wife and the puppet theatre were gone.

And so, it turned out, were Sparrow and Spud.

CHAPTER 2

Whilst Stick was engaged in a frantic search for Spud and Sparrow in the sweltering heat and the befuddled crowds of Bartholomew Fair, the rest of his gang of street urchins were waiting on Pickled Herring Stairs on the south side of the river for the tumblers to return with the promised Bartholomew's Day feast.

Since the start of the Great Heat back in July, the gutterlings had migrated to the banks of the river like a flock of starlings. They met up there when it was too hot to work, and to sleep of an evening. It was better than being fried like so many eggs on the pavements up town, though the stench from the mud was almost unbearable.

'It's so hot the toffs is calling it the Great Heat . . .' Tree lay back lazily on the cool stone step that she was sharing with her sister, Cess. Their long silver hair drifted over the steps like spilled mercury. In the gathering dusk, it looked as though shards of reflected moonshine had bounced up off the river.

'Great Stink, more like,' replied Cess.

'It were stinking high enough to knock down a horse,' Tree agreed.

After the departure of Fly, who had been the gutterlings' natural leader, Cess and Tree had taken over alongside Stick at the head of the gang. Everyone followed Stick without question, partly because he was the tallest, and partly because he always had the best plans. The sisters took a rather more motherly attitude to the job than Fly had, and it wasn't to everyone's taste. Bit too bossy, some of them said. Fly had enjoyed being in charge only because she could lead them all on wild larks and because everyone had hung on her stories, no matter how far-fetched.

Tree and Cess made their living as mudlarks, grubbing through putrid river mud in the hope of finding their fortune. So if *they* could smell something bad, the others knew it was time to listen up.

Bandy, the crossing-sweeper – so named on account of his knees that refused to meet in the middle – joined in. 'This cove dropped dead before my very eyes, just as I was sweeping my crossing, this arternoon. The heat got him by the throat, they said. Right bad for business, it was. Nobody wants to be stepping over a stiff.' He was indignant, having a sense of right and wrong every bit as strong as Spud's. But Bandy had stuck with sweeping crossings because he didn't mind doing a bit of flummery and flim-flam to butter up the customers.

Silence. An almost-full moon was rising over what was left of the drought-shrunken river. The chat was subdued this evening. Every night, this tattered band of tumblers and mudlarks and crossing-sweepers and flower-girls and horse-yobs huddled together to share a prigged pie and a begged crust and the narrow escapes of the day. But this evening – just like Stick had observed to the tumblers only a few hours before – something didn't feel right.

'Tumblers is late,' Tree observed.

'Too hot to tumble daytime, mebbe . . .' Cess suggested.

'They'll still be up the fair, codding the drunks out of their last bit of mint-sauce.' Bandy sounded envious.

'I hopes they brings back some nosh, like they promised . . .' Squinty, as they called him on account of his eyes, which *did* meet in the middle, unlike Bandy's knees, swept the crossing next to Bandy's. He didn't have much brains for business – or indeed for anything else – and Bandy kept an eye out for him so he didn't get bubbled out of what few tips he earned. But pickings had been poor for both of them all week. The mud was dried to dust, so there was nothing to sweep, and the toffs had taken themselves off to the country to escape the heat, so there was no one left to sweep for, neither.

At least here by the river, perched on Pickled Herring Stairs, under the iron girders of the bridge, the street urchins were safely out of sight of the crushers, who were always on the lookout for a reason to lock them up. But the gutterlings could still hear the heavy tread of the policemen's boots as they strode over the bridge above, rattling their night-sticks along the railings like a threat.

The gang's hiding place was opposite the rotten mouth of the Fleet, where it tipped its refuse into the Thames. The Fleet started as a swift and merry stream up in the high hills of Hampstead, where those who could afford it paid to breathe clean air, but by the time it got here it was slowed to a trickle of sewage.

The gutterlings watched as idle waves slopped sluggishly around a dead donkey, which had been rotting in the shallows for days – even the Thames had lost the will to wash away the city's filth.

17

'Ain't that the donkey what pulls Pardiggle's milk cart?' asked Bandy.

'Mebbe – it weren't looking too clever last week,' said Squinty.

'Looks a deal worse now,' Bandy observed.

'He don't half get through them donkeys,' Tree pointed out. 'Second one dead this year. Fly said as she'd seen what was left of the last one in her tiger's cage.'

'That varmint Pardiggle don't deserve no donkeys, way he treats them,' Cess said fiercely. She'd sooner be dead than own up to it, but Cess had a soft heart when it came to waifs and strays and indeed anything that needed her help. *Too soft for her own good, on these streets*, her sister often thought privately.

Silence again.

'Something don't smell right. And it ain't just that donkey.' Tree got to her feet. She was saying what everyone was thinking, and they all looked round uneasily as if they expected some mythological monster to rise from the earth.

'Even the toshers who work down the sewers is saying the city don't smell right.' Cess stood up and leaned on a metal railing next to Tree, as pale and thin as her sister. Sometimes it seemed like it was only the streaks of mud on their skin that made them visible.

'Even Lanky Bill . . .'

18

'Him what's been down them sewers since he could crawl . . .'

'Even he won't go down there no more.'

The pair of them often shared out words like they had always shared out any food that came their way. Neither finished a full sentence or a whole crust without making sure the other had had enough. The nuns had given them their saints' names – Teresa and Cecilia – and little else but thin fish-porridge and clouts about the head, until they were old enough to escape to the wild freedom of the streets. Neither one remembered a mother who might have told them who had come into the world first or even whether they was twins, 'cos neither one remembered a time without the other, either.

'Smells like sulphur, that's what he said. Bad eggs is what I call it . . .'

'He said it smelled like the Old Scratch was toasting . . .'

'. . . crumpets down there.'

It was then that the long lone figure of Stick loomed out of the shadows.

'You're . . .'

'. . . late!'

No one had ever seen Stick rattled about anything – he was the silent thinker, cool as a cucumber when times got tight. But there was something different in his gaunt face tonight. His eyes, as light and grey as drops of sea-water, had a haunted look in the moonlight.

'I been looking everywhere for Spud and Sparrow. They is gone.'

The gutterlings were on their feet in an instant, crowding round him, all rattling out questions at once.

'What do you mean, gone? Crushers nabbed them?'

'Was they dipping pockets?'

'Is they in quod?' If the police got you and you ended up behind the black walls of Newgate Prison, everyone knew there was only one way out – dancing from the gallows, on the end of a rope.

'I don't know. Something happened, up the fair.' Stick was never one to tell tall tales of an evening, in fact he was never one to say a single word more than was needful – so now they were all hanging on everything he said.

'What? What happened?' demanded Tree.

'It were like something belched, under the ground . . . and there was this stink . . . and everyone fell down like they was drunk as boiled owls . . .'

Bandy laughed, but Tree frowned and he stopped. Stick was still talking, like he was stuck in a nightmare he couldn't wake up from.

'. . . and when I looked round Spud and Sparrow was gone. Clean gone . . . it were like they been swallowed . . . swallowed into the ground . . .'

'Gammon!'

'You're bamming!'

'He's gone off his dot – it's the heat what's got to his head!'

Stick's face had filled with something that looked like dread, and the rest came out as a whisper. 'Or else they was snabbled by someone.'

His next words – *'There was this man . . .'* – got lost somewhere in the clamour that followed. Cess was the only one who caught what he'd said.

'Hold yer hush!' she hissed. 'Stick's not one to get in a tweak about nowt! Let him finish.'

But Stick was done. He just shook his head, and pushed his way through to take a seat on the steps. He didn't want to explain why the sight of that man had struck such terror into his soul. That would mean telling the story he had never told, not even to Fly, since he'd turned up on these streets from nowhere, all those years ago.

Subdued now, the flock of gutterlings settled back on the steps around him, waiting for someone to say something.

21

'Well, we all knows Spud and Sparrow ain't the first,' Bandy said at last. It was the truth that nobody had wanted to say out loud.

'What means you, they ain't the first?' came the frightened voice of a horse-yob who'd arrived from the country a few weeks before. He was taller even than Stick and he had freckles all over his face that made him look a foreigner to the street-pale gutterlings. He didn't even talk like them. Nobody knew him nor trusted him yet.

'There ain't many kinchen out on the streets, last few days,' said Bandy. 'They has gone missing – or else they is too scared to stay . . .'

They all knew what Bandy meant.

'Where be they all a-goon? Has they bin yaffled?' the horse-yob asked quickly. He looked more frightened than anyone.

'Why can't you talk proper King Billy's English like the rest of us?' demanded Cess.

Tree scowled. 'School,' she replied to the horse-yob, reluctantly. She didn't like all these questions from some Johnny-come-lately.

Everyone turned to stare at her.

'Don't be a loblolly – why would anyone go to school?' Squinty was having none of it.

22

'School's for toffs!' scoffed Bandy. 'We already knows everything we needs to know.'

'You kens stuff you bain't telling us!' The horse-yob wouldn't be silenced.

Tree and Cess looked at each other. It didn't seem like they'd been planning to share this juicy gobbet of news with anyone. But in the end Cess shrugged and picked up where Tree had left off. 'There's this woman – she's been coming round asking children to go with her . . .' she said, slowly.

'. . . she says as she's got this school in the country, and the childers will get three slap-up dinners a day . . .' added Tree.

'. . . and plum duff for pudding,' finished Cess.

'I'd go to school if it meant plum duff for pudding,' chipped in Squinty, who hadn't eaten since yesterday.

'That's why we didn't tell you!' snapped Tree.

'Cos we knew you'd go all daffy – running arter the plum pudding and never asking no questions . . .'

'. . . and never be seen no more!' finished Cess, in her darkest voice.

They all turned to Stick. Stick was the planner. He would know what was what. But he just sat staring at stuff nobody else could see. Everyone was getting more and more twitched at his silence.

At last Stick looked up and asked, 'What she look like, this woman?'

'A real cough-drop, she were. Right nasty bit of work.'

Cess nodded agreement with her sister. 'If it weren't for the promise of plum duff, nobody would be totty-headed enough to go with her.'

'But what did she look like?' Stick was impatient now.

'She were togged up like a lady – a real flash dona.'

'Yeah, posh togs, right enough – and tall – tall as Tyburn gallows.'

'And skinny as a shotten herring.'

'But she were a real beetroot-mug – with a nose like a parish pickaxe.'

Stick was pale as ash now and shivering. 'Blister me, not her too . . .' he whispered, so quiet nobody else heard. 'What's that wicked pair up to?'

After they thought all the other gutterlings were sound asleep, Tree and Cess lay whispering to each other, into the darkness.

'There's summat Stick ain't telling us,' said Cess. 'Summat he knows about that woman.'

24

'Stick's a deep one, all right,' Tree replied. 'Always kept his-self to his-self, hasn't he? Like – who even knows where he come from?'

'He just turned up that night, remember? Must've been 'least six summers gone.'

'Everyone else was born in the workhouse,' Tree went on.

'Or was brung up by the nuns, like us.'

'Beaten up by the nuns, more like!' Tree snorted.

'We all knew each other, though, didn't we?' persisted Cess. 'But Stick just popped up from nowhere – and not a soul had clapped eyes on him afore.'

'And he never said nowt about where he come from, not a sausage, not even to Fly.'

'And he were right fond of Fly . . .'

At last their voices trailed off into sleep, but Stick's eyes were still open. He had heard everything they'd said, but he said nothing. He wasn't ready to tell.

CHAPTER 3

It was blue o'clock in the morning when Stick stood up and slunk away from Pickled Herring Stairs, leaving the rest of the gutterlings curled up together like stray kittens on the steps. Nobody saw him go.

He hadn't slept. Whenever he'd closed his eyes those faces were there, leering at him like the gargoyles that grinned from the gutter of every city church. Beetroot-faced, beak-nosed, wicked. The man as broad as the woman was skinny.

The evil he thought he'd left behind him many years before was now prowling these streets, where he'd thought he was safe.

Something told him that all the palaver and comflobstigation beneath Bartlemy Fair the day before

26

– and the disappearance of Spud and Sparrow – were connected with the man who had just walked out of his past.

And now there was the woman for him to worrit over, too – the one Tree and Cess were talking about. What did she want with the street urchins she had snabbled?

Stick had to face the evil. He had to find out what they were up to. Nobody else knew what he knew about that man and that woman. It was up to him to stop them. But where to start? As he'd lain there in the darkness, after Tree and Cess had stopped whispering about him, the only plan he could think up was to go back to where he had last seen Spud and Sparrow. Maybe there was some clue he had missed?

So in the end he had got up, and now here he was, dodging into shadows and hardly daring to breathe as the night-watch passed by, calling out the hour. 'Three o'clock o' the morning, and all's well!'

'Fat lot you knows,' Stick called after him, but very quietly.

As he passed under the city gate, a sudden flurriment of dark wings above his head made him jump and look up. He ducked as a pair of pigeons that had been fighting over a roost flapped away.

21

'Blimey!' He'd never before noticed the huge silver and scarlet stone dragon that leered down from the arch, breathing fire from its gaping mouth. He'd heard tell that it was the ancient guardian of the city, but it didn't look too trustworthy to Stick.

'Cor, love-a-lily-white-duck!' Stick whispered up to it. 'You looks like a wicked old scorcher, all right.' It made him feel even more uneasy, as if danger was lurking all around him. And once he'd seen that dragon, he kept seeing more, on every bollard and every street sign.

'Blimey, them dragons is everywhere . . .' From the glint in their eyes, it wasn't clear to Stick what their game was. Were they there to protect the city – or were they planning to burn it merrily to the ground, first chance they got?

Stick wasn't used to being on his own, without Spud and Sparrow jabbering nonsense at his side. Gutterlings like them rarely risked being out alone in the dark, if they knew what was good for them. And he wasn't used to the silence of the city at night. It was the silence of many hundreds sleeping, but it was also the silence of many thousands dead. The dead whose bones lay buried and forgotten beneath his feet.

He found the words of what might have been a prayer popping into his head. It was a prayer that someone he had

28

loved a long time ago had repeated with him, as they kneeled together by a snow-white bedside . . .

But he stuffed all that firmly back into the cupboard in the back of his head, because in his experience good stuff could hurt just as much as bad.

The dark dome of St Paul's loomed down over him as he stole up Sermon Lane, through Angel Court and around Amen Corner and past a dozen churches. There was a fusty smell from the dank graveyards, more noticeable at night when there was no spicy breeze from the sleeping pickle-factories across the river in Bermondsey.

Stick carefully avoided, as all wise gutterlings did, the black walls of Newgate Prison. He crept along narrow back alleys until he stood under the great Gate of Heaven between the church of Bartlemy the Great and the meat stalls of Smithfield. They called it the Gate of Heaven because it was the way into Bartlemy's Hospital, and most people never came out again, unless it was feet first in a wooden box.

It was near this spot that he'd last seen Spud and Sparrow, and part of him was hoping he'd find them here now, waiting for him. He imagined them snacking on a prigged snossidge – as Spud called them – ready to roast him something wicked about his worriting.

Stick found a wall where he felt safe and leaned back against the still-warm brick. He'd not stopped shivering all night, even though the sweltering temperature had hardly dropped. The loneliness of the pre-dawn streets had steeped fear deep into his bones. He wasn't used to this quiet, without the street-cries and the clatter of carts on the cobbles. A soot-stiffened sparrow, up early to beat its flock-mates to the overnight crumbs, was all he had for company.

Where you gone, you daft pair of loblollies? Stick scolded Spud and Sparrow in his head, as he took out his pipe to think.

At last Smithfield turned pink in the dawn light and started to wake up for the last day of Bartlemy Fair. Street-sellers rattled in with their carts and the show-masters blearily began opening up their caravans after a long, late night.

A nearby bill-board was offering a peek at the Smallest Woman, not more than eighteen inches high, and the Tallest Man, together with a Living Skellington and a Four-Legged Duck. Four shows for a penny, and cheap at the price.

On the first day of the fair, Sparrow had been keen to blow any earnings on a visit to the Smallest Woman, but Spud had said it was only because he wanted to see someone smaller than him for a change, and maybe they should set

30

up a show for themselves and sell Sparrow for a farthing a look. 'Arter all, nobody's going to pay a full ha'penny to cop a look at Sparrow,' he'd said.

Stick grinned at the image of Sparrow headbutting Spud in retaliation, but his grin soon faded because neither of them was there to share the joke.

'Blimey!' Stick edged sideways nervously as the lock rattled on the door of the Ghost Caravan next to him. It was a relief when it was only the proprietor who emerged, very much alive. He was naked to the waist but for a pair of red braces which were straining to hold in rolls of pale blubber.

The man was cursing the dawn and rubbing the rusty bristles on his chin like he hoped he could rub away his beard and save himself the pother of a shave.

The smell of the spiced sausages heating up on the first breakfast stalls drifted over and reminded Stick he hadn't eaten since that shared twist of fried fish.

'Saveloys, just up! Get them hissing hot! Hot as they come!' the saveloy woman was shouting.

Drabbit it, Stick thought. *I is nibblish hungry . . .* He jingled the few coppers in his pocket that the tumblers had taken the day before. *But it don't feel right to spend their dibs.*

31

Stick always looked after the money for the three of them, but he never spent it just on himself. Being the tallest he was less likely to get mugged by the bully boys from Clare Market. 'Besides,' as Spud had once pointed out, 'you're the only one with pockets that ain't more hole than pocket.'

But in the end hunger got the better of him. *Any road*, he reasoned with himself, as he sidled over to the stall, *you don't rightly know when you'll see Spud and Sparrow again, if you does ever see them ag*— He wouldn't let himself finish the thought, even in his head.

'Got any fall-downs, missus?' he asked the woman, as he handed over the coins. It was always worth a try for the cheaper bits that had been on the floor, which nobody else would touch.

'There you go, my buttercup!' She sneaked him some broken bits of saveloy.

He recognised the woman from the first day of the fair, when the tumblers had put on a few somersaults just for her after she'd given them all an extra scoop of saloop that was stuck to the bottom of the can.

'Saloop an' all?' she asked him now, as he bit down on the sausage, grease dripping down his chin.

Stick considered, tempted by the thought of the hot, sweet, creamy drink. He nodded and grunted, his mouth too full to speak.

She took his penny and dolloped out an extra-thick helping. Like the bags of mystery and penny-puzzlers that passed for sausages on these streets, nobody rightly knew what was in it, but as Spud would have said, it was a real gum-tickler.

'Big spender, today, my pippin?'

It was a question, and Stick stiffened. He didn't like questions. But she was still smiling. *Regular gigglemug, this one!* thought Stick, determined not to encourage her by smiling back.

'Where's the other little tykes?' she asked.

The saveloy gone too quick to avoid answering, Stick gave her a long cautious look over the rim of his cup. Her cheeks were rosy with the steam from the saloop can, and there was a softness about her blue eyes that was in danger of making him trust her.

'Dunno,' he mumbled. You had to be careful with words. Words could be turned into weapons, if they fell into the wrong hands. But she was still smiling, and he needed help if he was going to find the tumblers.

'You ain't seen them, has you?' He forced the question out quickly, before he could change his mind.

'Not since you tumbled for us, day afore yesterday, pet,' she replied. Her face had changed, like she was already dreading what he might say next. 'Why?'

In for a penny, in for a pound, thought Stick. He had to trust someone.

'They has disappeared.' He plunged on. 'When there were all that bobbery and ruckus, yesterday, you know?'

She nodded so vigorously that her cap fell off into the saloop can. By the stains, Stick judged it wasn't the first time it had been in there.

'Fair frighted me into convulsions, all that did!' she said, fishing her cap out and shaking it off.

'Well, when I looked for them arterwards, they was gone.' Stick told her. He watched her face carefully as he said it. 'Can't find them nowhere.'

The woman turned away quickly to give the saloop a stir it didn't need. When she looked back, her smiles had been wiped away by what looked like fear.

'Stop looking for them, love. No good can come of it.' Her voice came out as a hiss, like she didn't want to be overheard. 'I sent my kinchen away to me mam in the country. If you've any sense, get out of this godforsaken city, before you're disappeared along with the others.'

She stuffed a whole saveloy into his hand. 'Now get along with you!'

She turned away quickly before Stick could ask any more questions. The man in charge of the Wonders of the World

34

show had come over to order three and a quarter breakfasts for himself, the Smallest Woman, the Tallest Man and the Living Skellington. And some crusts for the Four-Legged Duck.

Stick's belly was fit to bust as he wandered through the thickening crowd of the fair, but there was no way he was going to save that saveloy for later. If there was grub to be had, you scoffed it – that was the rule.

But it wasn't just over-eating that was making him queasy. And it wasn't just the mood of the crowd, either. It was fear.

It was going to be another broiler of a day. The crowd was twitchy. Word had spread about the commotion of yesterday, and even though it was early, people were stuffing down pies and pastries and downing flagons of beer like it was their last meal on earth. 'Can't take it with you!' was the toast at every overcrowded alehouse he passed.

Stick began to notice an uneasy motion beneath his feet. He'd never been at sea, but he reckoned it was not unlike being on board a ship. The closest he'd come was when he almost got on that boat and sailed away to Lord knows where with Fly and her tiger, and all the animals they'd freed from the menagerie.

What larks that was, Fly! he thought wistfully. But there wasn't time to talk to Fly now, because he realised that the

35

earth was indeed moving, very gently. And once he'd noticed that, he realised that it was shifting as regularly as a heartbeat. In fact, he could have sworn that the earth was breathing.

Or that something very large was breathing underneath it.

'Clobber me!' Stick whispered to his toes. 'What in mussy's name is down there?'

He set off, pushing his way through the heaving fairground, eyes fixed firmly on the cobbles, which were rippling like pebbles in the undertow. He wasn't sure what he was looking for. But he knew now, clear as day-glim, that the answer to what had happened to Spud and Sparrow – and the reason that evil pair from his past had come to London – lay beneath his feet.

'Watch where you is going, clod-pate!' Curses and blows rained on Stick's head as he stumbled into food stalls and bumped into a fire-breathing juggler, sending his torches flying. But nobody was steady on their feet now. There was a stink of sweat as the crowd grew ever more uneasy and bad-tempered. It was still early but heat was already beating down from above and rising from beneath the ground, and Bartlemy Fair was as hot as a griddle-pan.

Then at last he saw it.

'What you staring at, goggles?'

A belligerent old slubberdegullion was lying down against a wall for a little snoozle in the sun. But it wasn't him that Stick was staring at.

There was a narrow crack next to the man, between the wall and the ground. It was barely noticeable, but it was there.

Mebbe Spud and Sparrow rolled down there, in all that pandalorum yesterday . . . Stick thought, because it was close to where he'd last seen them, near the Gate of Heaven. *Though for all I know it might lead down to Hell,* Stick thought uneasily. Maybe he was going to have to start believing in all that stuff after all.

As he watched the crack, he realised it was gently opening and closing, in time with the movement of the earth. And also in time with the sound of breaths that he couldn't help hearing now, despite the hubbub of the fair.

'I ain't going down there . . . I ain't going down there . . .' It took him a while to realise he was saying it out loud.

Stick had his reasons for hating the idea of being shut up in dark places. He had his reasons for dreading going underground. All reasons that he didn't want to think about. And all reasons that should have made him run a million miles before crawling into that crack in the earth. But he knew he had to do it.

'I ain't going down there.'

He was still saying it as he took a deep breath and pushed himself down through that crack. Down into darkness.

CHAPTER 4

There was no splash, no accompanying stink. *So I ain't landed in the sewer,* thought Stick.

But where was he?

Wherever he was, it was dark, and very, very hot. *But if this is Hell,* he consoled himself, *it's a lot quieter than the preachers let on.*

He must have slid down ten feet, but there was nothing underfoot that felt like the crumpled bodies of Spud and Sparrow, which is what he had been dreading most.

So help me, I has been and gone and done it now! he thought. This wasn't his usual way of going about things. He was a lad who liked to take a good long look before he leaped.

He gazed up, but it was clear that there was no way back. The trickle of light from the crack revealed only the smooth, sheer wall he'd slid down.

Being a tumbler by trade, Stick had landed light and soundless as a feather on his feet, but he sensed that something had heard him, and that the something was waiting for his next move.

His eyes were starting to adjust to the low light, but he couldn't tell whether it was something very large that was trying to seem very small, or something very small that was trying to seem very large. He couldn't hear anything breathing now. He reckoned it was holding its breath, just like he was holding his.

One of us is going to have to take a breath in a minute, Stick thought. *Or we'll both end up brown bread.*

'Gadzooks! Who dares to wake me?'

Stick jumped like a jellied eel. Even to a lad who liked to deal in facts, the sound could only have been described as a roar. Not a loud roar, but loud enough to be uncomfortable. And hot enough to be uncomfortable, too.

Something long and snakelike whipped out at him from the shadows and slithered over his skin, leaving a trail of slime behind it. It felt horribly like a large tongue.

Almost like it was tasting me . . . Stick shivered.

And then the snakey thing disappeared and there was a noise that sounded rather like someone smacking a pair of – large – lips.

Stick backed away, but he didn't get far before he hit that wall again. There was nowhere to go. He kept quiet and tried to do what he did best. Think.

The roar had put him in mind of Fly's tiger. But he pushed that thought away, because meeting a tiger what didn't try to eat you but even let you ride on its back – that was something that only happened to people like Fly. Not to a lad who dealt in facts, like himself.

He'd had a suspicion, back then, that Fly could talk to her tiger, but he'd always tried to ignore that, because it wasn't possible. Besides, when her tiger roared, it didn't feel so hot that it hurt. No, this definitely wasn't a tiger. It was something else entirely.

But he wasn't ready to hold a conversation with whatever it was just yet. It might, after all, not be real. A figment of what he'd heard people call 'imagination'.

Stick tried alternately squinting and then opening his eyes very wide, but he still couldn't make anything out in the shadows.

He sniffed. There was a strong smell now of burned dust and rotten eggs.

'What the devil are you?' He hadn't meant to say it out loud, but it somehow slipped out.

'Devil?' There was a long snort, so hot that Stick could feel it singeing the fraying edges of his kecks. The voice of whatever it was went on.

'I hope you are not fool enough to hold with that superstitious nonsense? I assure you that I have been down here a very long time, boy, and never even had the least whiff of Beelzebub.'

Stick slapped at what was left of his smouldering trousers and took a deep breath.

'It ain't real,' he told himself, quietly. 'It's just a bit of sausage what's disagreed with you, and set up a rumpus in your chitterlings!'

'Sausage?' A long, scaly, dusty snout of an indeterminate colour was suddenly thrust into his thin chest, knocking him back against the wall. 'Did you say sausage?'

There was a loud eager sniff, a sniff that almost inhaled Stick's remaining rags from off his back. It was like being sniffed by an omnibus.

'You don't happen to have any of that deliciousness about your person? If you do, it might postpone my need to eat you.'

There was a wistful look in the bottomless yellow eye that was now glistening next to Stick. The eye was as high as he was. He could only see one – he assumed there was a matching one on the other side of that long snout.

Stick was uncomfortably aware that the snout bore a close resemblance to the snout worn by that creature he'd seen on the top of the city gate. But he wasn't going to say the name of that mythical beast out loud just yet. Because that was a fiction and Stick preferred facts.

'No, I ain't got no sausages,' he replied and then wished he hadn't, because it could only encourage this figment of his indigestion to keep talking to him.

'Shame.' A long sigh, which was in danger of igniting Stick's kecks again. Then, 'I had a sausage once. It rolled right down a grate and into my mouth. So good! What the bejeepers do they put in them?'

'Blame me if I knows.' Stick had to admit that this was now a conversation. 'Nobody knows. That's why they calls them "bags of mystery". "Penny-puzzlers". 'Cos they is probably stuffed full of bow-wow mutton.'

'Humph.' A long – warm – sigh of disappointment. 'I don't remember when I last had a nice snack.'

Stick didn't like the way those powerful jaws snapped shut on the word 'snack', and he hesitated to raise the subject, but it was, after all, what had brought him down here.

'When you says you ain't eaten for a while . . .' he began delicately. He hesitated again and went on, 'There weren't two puny little whey-faced lads what might have dropped down here yesterday, what you might have snacked on and forgotten about? They goes by the names of Spud and Sparrow,' he went on. 'But mebbe they didn't have time for introductions? Not much meat on them, I know, but I was fond of them, as it happens.'

'Not that I recollect . . .' A pause, and then it added, as if

44

it was reminding itself, 'In any case, I don't eat children.'

The pupil of the eye next to him narrowed, to examine him more closely. 'But I'm not sure that you would count. Far too big for a child, I think . . .?'

'They always said I was tall for my age,' Stick said quickly.

The beast half closed the eye. 'I'm getting a little peckish, I must say.' It was looking decidedly shifty. 'I haven't eaten a soul for an absolute age.'

It yawned, its top jaw stretching to the tunnel roof. It was then that Stick noticed the bedraggled remains of what looked suspiciously like the stripy Punch and Judy puppet booth snaggled round one of its very sharp teeth.

What happened to Punch and his missus – and the cove what does the puppet show? Stick thought of asking, but decided it wasn't wise.

He reckoned it was best not to ask too many questions about the missing puppets – and their puppet-master – but it did leave him with the strong feeling that this beast wasn't to be trusted. And he noticed that its mouth was rather closer to him now than it had been at the start of this conversation.

'Look, mister, missus, whatever . . . would you mind backing off a little, it's a bit . . .'

'A little odiferous?' it suggested.

Stick looked blank.

'You think my breath smells?'

Stick shrugged. He hadn't liked to mention it, but there was a definite hint of bad eggs underlying the smell of burned trousers.

The snout withdrew with a snort so offended it was in danger of singeing Stick's eyebrows. 'Unforgiveably rude! The boy has the manners of a hedge-fish. And to not recognise a lady when he meets one!'

'Beg pardon, ma'am,' Unlike Spud, Stick was well-accustomed to buttering up toffs, and it seemed like a good idea not to cause offence to a creature that was as touchy as a Lucifer match. 'I can't see you in all your glory, down here in the dark. I bet you are a real sight for sore eyes, if I could only cop a proper look at you.'

It was a shameless bit of flummery, but it seemed to work.

'Ah!' Another sigh, more wistful even than the sausage sigh. 'How right you are, child! If only I could show you! But there isn't room to swing a cow down here.'

The eye next to Stick suddenly brimmed over. 'If you could only have seen how magnificent I was in my prime.

46

Swooping across the earth beside my sisters . . . quartering the globe between sunrise and sunset . . . striking fear into mortal hearts . . .'

'So how did you end up in a hole?'

The eye dried up and glared at Stick. 'I got stuck. Stuck underground.'

'Stuck?'

'Yes, stuck, boy! It happens. Even to the best of us.'

Stick had completely forgotten that he didn't believe in this creature now. It was like listening to one of Fly's tallest tales. He just wanted to hear how it ended.

What Stick didn't realise was how much there was still to come, and how it would become his story too.

'Go on, missus – I mean, ma'am,' he urged. 'What happened?'

'I fell asleep. After a large meal.' The words were slow and reluctant now. Almost, you might say, embarrassed. 'I ate too much.'

'Everyone deserves a blow-out, now and then,' Stick said, encouragingly.

'But while I was asleep, the ground shifted and the earth fell in. When I woke up the mouth of the cave was blocked, and my sisters were buried somewhere deep amongst the rocks. I could hear them calling to me. But gradually their cries faded away. I never saw them again.'

Great rivulets of tears spilled out over Stick, and hissed and steamed gently, leaving salt-crusted stains on the hot ground.

'I have been alone under the earth ever since. Waiting for a knight in shining armour to come and end it all.' A quick turn of the snout suddenly almost knocked Stick off his feet. 'Your name isn't George, is it? Saint George, that is?'

Both eyes were blazing down on him now and he thought he could see flames flickering in the depths of the black pupils. Was there a heart in there, or just burning embers?

Stick hesitated. 'No, ma'am. Just Stick, that's all. Plain Stick.' There was another name, but it was in the back of that cupboard, along with all the rest of the stuff he wouldn't let himself remember.

There was a sigh that might have been relief or disappointment. 'Ah, well. Never mind. I just thought the long wait might have been over at last. If my memory serves me correctly, it is traditionally only a knight that can talk to a dragon. And only a knight that can slay a dragon. A true knight, who is pure of heart. But I admit, you don't look much like a knight. Or a saint. Too dirty, for one thing.'

48

'And my togs ain't right neither, ma'am,' pointed out Stick, who had seen one or two suits of armour in another life, though he wasn't saying where. 'I ain't got much in the way of trousers, let alone what's needful for a full-blown knight.'

'No, of course. I see that.' Another sigh.

She don't half do a lot of sighing – full of the mulligrabs, she is! thought Stick.

The blaze in the eyes had begun to fade, and the scaly snout sank to the ground. 'I am tired. I am not used to all this idle chatter.' A lazy, leathery eyelid slid half-way down the eye next to Stick. But she didn't stop talking. 'My time has passed.' Another sigh. 'I should have died with my sisters, instead of being left alone to cower here under the earth. It is not right. It is not in the nature of a Werme to cower . . .'

'A worm?' Stick still couldn't see much of the beast he was talking to, but he would never have put it down as a worm.

'Tch!' The eyelid flew up with a sharp tut of impatience. 'Werme is the ancient and honourable name for my kind. What a common fool might call . . . a dragon.'

It was what Stick had suspected for some time. He was banged up down here with a dragon. A living, breathing

49

– and talking – dragon. But for a common fool who liked things he understood, it was a difficult idea to swallow.

'I'd heard tell as all the dragons was dead,' he ventured, tactful as he could.

'I am the last of my race.' Yet another sigh. 'Others fear being condemned to death, but I am condemned to life.'

Blimey, she's mopey as a wet hen, thought Stick.

The cobbles creaked above Stick's head as the dragon's ribs rose and fell. The next sigh was very sleepy, and the roar was dimmed to a whisper.

'The heart is a muscle over which no living thing has any control, my child. That is the greatest tragedy in life – you cannot make your own heart stop beating.'

'You can make a heart break,' said Stick, who had seen it done.

'Fairy tales!' came a drowsy mumble.

'Hark who's talking!' retorted Stick.

But the mythical beast was snoring.

CHAPTER 5

While Stick was holding a conversation with a dragon below Bartlemy Fair, Tree and Cess were conducting a council of war back at Pickled Herring Stairs. It was hotter even than the day before, and the band of gutterlings had given up any attempt at work and returned to the river in the vain hope of a breath of fresh air.

'Has anyone clapped eyes on Stick?' demanded Tree.

They all shook their heads. Nobody had seen hide nor hair of Stick, though Tree and Cess had set up a search for him as soon as they woke at day-glim and found him gone.

Cess turned back to Bandy. 'Did you put the word about on the crossings to watch out for him?'

Bandy shook his head miserably. 'I tried, Cess, but there ain't enough of us working to get the word passed on. It's too hot, there's no toffs to give us tips and everyone is too perishing hungry to sweep.'

The heat had broken the network of spies on each street crossing, which normally kept the gutterlings informed about anything that twitched, anywhere in the city.

'Don't say Stick's been snabbled like all the rest?' piped up Tiddy Doll. She was a flower-seller, and they called her Tiddy Doll, because she was barely big enough to amount to a whole child. She'd been out selling flowers so late the night before she'd not made it back to Pickled Herring Stairs, but had curled up to sleep in a basket up at Covent Garden instead.

Tiddy was as delicate as a china doll, with blue eyes the colour of the bunches of the violets she sold in the spring. But nobody would have bought a doll with a face as thin and pinched with hunger as hers. She was so small she was always looking up, which usually gave her a hopeful look, like a flower turning its head to seek out the sun. But now she was looking more scared than hopeful.

'Don't fret, Tiddy.' Cess put her arm round her. 'Stick's got all his buttons on – he's not buffle-headed enough to fall for a load of old flim-flam.' But she looked a lot less sure than she was trying to sound.

Tree was looking round. She turned to glare at Bandy. 'Never mind all that – where's Squinty?'

Bandy squirmed but there was nobody to hide behind with so few gutterlings left now on Pickled Herring Stairs.

'He's gone.'

'I can see that he's gone. I wouldn't be asking where he was, if he was standing here in front of me, now would I?' snapped Tree. 'What I asked was, *where's* he gone?' But she looked like she knew the answer already.

'That flash dona – that lady with the conk like a ship's rudder – the one you was talking about . . .'

'Don't tell me – she promised him plum duff and all the trimmings, and now he's gone off with her! How could you let him go?' Cess scolded, but her voice was shaking.

'Even arter we warned him, and all!' Tree shook her head in disbelief.

'Don't be so down on him, Tree. I know he ain't all there, most of the time, but a boy can't live on air-pie!' Bandy came to the defence of his fellow crossing-sweeper. 'We ain't made a farthing, last few days, what with the swells all going off to the country, and not a drop of mud to be swept nowhere!'

'Bandy's right – it's too hot to work – all me flowers is wilted before I can sell them,' chipped in Tiddy Doll.

'But look – Stick and Spud and Sparrow gone, and now

53

Squinty – there's hardly none of us left!' Tree snapped back. 'Count up!'

Counting was a problem for most of them, rarely having had to count past sixpence, which was a fortune few had ever possessed at one time. But there were only five of them left, so they could see she was right. Apart from Tree, Cess, Bandy and Tiddy Doll, there was only the horse-yob, who nobody really knew. He was still hanging about like he was looking for a horse to hold.

'What's she doing with them?' whispered Tiddy.

Fear was spreading like spilled treacle.

'We needs a plan,' said Cess.

'But Stick ain't here!' Tiddy Doll's voice was wobbly as a badly set junket.

'Where's he gone?' Bandy was starting to irritate Cess and her sister.

'Stop asking questions we don't know the answers to!' Tree snapped.

'How is I supposed to know what you don't know?' he retorted, but not loud enough for her to hear, because nobody wanted a lashing from the sharp edge of Tree's tongue.

Silence. The waves of the turning tide slapped sluggishly against the dead donkey, as listless as everything else in the oppressive heat.

'I reckon Stick knows who that woman is,' Cess said. 'I was watching his mug last night. He looked right scared, like he knew her from somewhere – somewhere before . . .'

'Somewhere before he came here,' Tree suggested.

Cess nodded. 'Me and Tree, we was trying to recall where Stick come from. Does anyone remember him, from the workhouse?'

Heads shaking all round.

'He just turned up one day and started chucking handsprings on the street,' said Bandy. 'And then it were like he'd always been here.'

'But he weren't always here, were he? Not like the rest of us.'

'Mebbe wherever he come from, that's where she's from too.'

It was then that the horse-yob piped up.

'I ken where he be from.'

The horse-yob hadn't said anything much worth listening to before, and they all turned and stared. He blushed under his mop of ginger curls. The bright freckles he'd brought with him, fresh from the country, were starting to fade. His face was taking on the same street pallor as the faces of the gutterlings. Life in the city didn't suit freckles.

'I has seen him afore,' he went on. 'But he bain't half so tall then, nor half so dirty.'

He fell silent, turning his cap nervously round and round in his hands like he was plucking a dead pigeon.

'Spit it out, then!' Tree said grudgingly. It took a while for an outsider to earn the right to speak.

'He were just a tiddler, and I was too, but I reckon it were him all right. He were all togged up in a velvet jacket and pantaloons.'

Bandy snorted a disbelieving snort. 'Stick in pantaloons! He ain't barely got two legs to his kecks.'

But the horse-yob was on a roll, now he'd started, and he wasn't stopping until he was done. 'He were sitting in a swanky trot-box, looking out the windy, alongside some big cove with a beetroot-mug and a pickaxe for a conk.'

'Sounds just like that woman – she were a right old hatchet-face!' exclaimed Cess.

'Only she weren't big,' Tree pointed out. 'She were as skinny as a rasher of wind.'

'Last night Stick were muttering summat about some cove he'd seen at Bartlemy Fair same time as Spud and Sparrow disappeared,' remembered Cess. 'He looked like he'd frightened the bejeepers out of him. Like he knew him from somewhere . . .'

56

A long look went round the gutterlings – they were taking a silent vote on whether to trust the horse-yob. They all knew each other so well that nobody needed to say anything. Tree could see the answer in everyone's eyes. She nodded.

'So where is this place?' she demanded.

'It be in the country.' The horse-yob was looking scared, but the gutterlings looked plain terrified when he mentioned the country. None of them had ever stepped foot outside the city gates, and they knew for a plain fact that the joskins and splodgers who lived in the country had two heads and ate nowt but turnips.

'That pair have made it a real bad place. That be why I come here. It bain't safe,' he added. 'My ma made me run away, 'cos the childers kept disappearing. Half a dozen of them been yaffled, by the time I left.'

'Mebbe they've run out of children in the country?' guessed Bandy. He'd not much idea how big the country was, but he was certain sure it couldn't be as big as London. 'So they're coming here to snabble the kinchen instead?'

'But what is they doing with them all?' whispered Tiddy Doll again.

'I don't know,' said Cess. 'But I'll lay a farthing to a flounder they ain't stuffing their silly snouts with figgy pudding and plum duff!'

57

'So what does we do now?' The horse-yob sounded doubtful.

'I wish Fly was here. She'd know what to do,' said Bandy. But he said it very quietly.

'I wish Stick was here.' Tiddy was trembling and Cess gave her a squeeze. Everyone was looking at Tree, who had a face like thunder. She didn't like their leadership being questioned. She stood up.

'We needs to go to the country and find them,' she declared, in a voice nobody was about to argue with.

58

CHAPTER 6

Less than a mile away, under Smithfield market, Stick was leaning against a wall of stone that felt reassuring real. The beast was still snoozing.

He took out his pipe and stuck it in his mouth. It was how he thought best, with that pipe in his mouth. He never had any tobacco in it, but if he had it would have been smouldering in the heat by now.

Above his head, through a grate, he could hear the cries of the stall-holders and the laughter of the crowd getting into the last-day-of-the-holiday spirit.

'Eels-alive-oh!'

'Sheep's feet! Get them hot!'

'Diddle diddle dumplings, ho!'

Down here the only sounds were gentle, regular snores from the dragon.

'Shifty old scorcher,' he muttered, clamping his teeth down on his pipe. 'I still ain't convinced she's not gobbled down Sparrow and Spud. I reckon she ain't that reliable, when it comes to truth-telling. Mind you, she might have clean forgot, with a belly that size. '

Stick peered closer. 'Mebbe she's sat on them and not twigged.' He could see better now he had been down here for a while.

The dusty expanse of her scaly skin seemed to stretch for ever. It was the colour of old grass before the frost takes it back into the earth for the winter. The beast was so large, the only bit he could see clearly was the snout.

The snout had rows of sharp teeth on each side, same as the corcodile what had snapped up a sweepling when it went for a wash in the Serpentine, according to the story Fly had told him. Above her mouth, the dragon had a great forehead, craggy as a cliff-face, that reached right up to the roof.

The closest he'd ever been to a beast this big was when he went to see the bones of a creature they'd put on show at some toff's house up town. Half London had coughed up a shilling a time to see it. The tumblers had only got a gander at it by shimmying up the drainpipes and hanging upside down off the windysills.

'It ain't nowt but a heap of old bones!' Spud had scoffed, when they'd peered through the windows, high above the heads of the noodles who were queuing up to pay through the nose. 'How come they can cod them all out of a shilling, just to get a gander at that?'

Putting it on show hadn't seemed right to Stick. *It ain't respectful, somehow*, he'd thought. It had been bigger even than the jumbos he and Fly had rescued from the menagerie. He had stared in silent wonder, filled with the mystery of such a beast waddling up Ludgate Hill.

Cor, there was a right hullabaloo over them bones, Stick remembered now. *Whoever dug them up must have made a pretty penny for themselves. What did the toffs call it? Megy-lo-snorus, that's it.* He looked at his new companion. *Well, 'snorus' would be right enough for you!*

In the trickle of daylight leaking through the gratings, he could make out that he and the dragon were sharing a scraped-out hollow in the stone foundations of some ancient building, long disappeared above. The space was barely wide and high enough to allow her room to breathe.

No wonder it were getting bumpy up there, with her rattling about down here, he thought. *I needs to stop her getting too*

rampageous, or the whole fair'll be down here on top of us, and I'll never find out what's happened to Spud and Sparrow!

He chewed on his pipe some more. 'I needs a plan,' he said quietly to himself. Stick had never been a seat-of-the-pants kind of person, like Fly was. He preferred to line up his facts like sprats on a plate.

'Leaving aside that I is stuck in a hole with a mythical creature what clearly can't exist . . .' He still didn't like to

say 'dragon' out loud. 'What is the facts of the matter?' He took out his pipe and tamped down some imaginary tobacco with his thumb, then he clamped it firmly back between his teeth.

'Fact one. Spud and Sparrow either got shook down here and ended up with that beast, or that cove's knocked them on the bonce with his umbyrelly and took them away in that big bag of his.'

A shudder shook Stick's thin frame before he could stop it. It was clear from his face that in his opinion, the man with the umbrella was the worse of those two evils.

'Fact two. If they fell down here, they has more than likely been eaten by old gobble-guts over there. Or they has been squashed flat as a griddle-cake under her belly. Or they managed to creep past her down that tunnel somehow.

'Fact three. This old scorcher can't have been squirrelled away down here for centuries, or London would be burned to a frazzle by now. She must have come here from somewhere else in the last few days, and that's why it's got so perishing hot. So that there tunnel must lead to that somewhere else, wherever it is.'

Stick took a few steps forwards. 'Mebbe Spud and Sparrow skedaddled up the tunnel when they twigged who they had for company?'

But his view down the tunnel was blocked by the dragon's belly, and as he tried to peer around it to get a better look he bumped into a taloned foot the size of a cart-wheel. The eyelid next to him flew up.

'What's your game, gutter-boy?' she snapped. 'Creeping off to leave me alone again? You've only just got here!'

That tongue whipped out again and twined itself tight

around Stick's legs. This time it was pulling him towards her mouth.

Stick gasped. *Now I'm for it!*

There was a worrying amount of drool dribbling out between her teeth, and Stick recognised the gleam in her eyes. It was a gleam of greed – the same gleam as Spud got in his eyes before he sank his teeth into a meat pie.

He thought quickly. *What did Fly do when she fell into the tiger's cage?*

Her answer came into his head, like she was there beside him. *I just kept him talking – I reckoned that, leastways, as long as he were talking he couldn't be chomping on me . . .*

'I were just trying to cop a look at your tail,' Stick blustered. 'I ain't never seen a dragon's tail afore.'

There was a long moment, and Stick was so close to her eye he reckoned he could see the argument going on in her head. *Eat him or talk to him?*

In the end, it seemed that talking won. Her tongue loosened its grip on his legs and snaked back behind her teeth.

'I told you already, you addle-pate, you mutton-head, you blithering nick-ninny! Don't you get it? I can't show you my tail because I'm stuck! I can't move!'

She tried to lurch to her feet and her head hit the roof. 'God's wounds! My head!' One huge foot stamped down

65

just inches from his ear. 'God's bodikins! My foot!'

Overhead, in Smithfield, there was a clattering and a commotion as the earth shifted. Stalls collapsed and women screamed and fainted. Then there was silence. Bartlemy Fair had been brought to a terrified halt once more.

Something that was more like a giggle than a snort erupted from the beast's nostrils.

'Oh, hark at them, how they fuss! That was nothing! I could show them!'

'Best not!' Stick said hastily, before she could give the roof another heave. So much for keeping her calm. But at least he'd distracted her, and the gleam of greed had gone from her eyes. 'You don't want to make such a pother and flustration that they come poking their noses down here, do you?'

'No . . . no . . . perhaps not.' A ton of dragon subsided back to the ground. 'That's why I came here, after all.'

'What do you mean, came here?' asked Stick, quickly. 'I thought you said you'd been stuck here for centuries?'

'No, no, you clod-pate, you maggot-brain, not here! You have it all topsy-turvy.'

One minute she talks like a toff, next she's cursing like a Billingsgate fishwife, thought Stick.

'I came here to get away from—' There was a hesitation.

66

A quick correction. 'I came here to get some peace.'

Was that fear? What was it that she did not want to tell him?

'I do so love how the blood drips down here from Smithfield, don't you?' She'd changed the subject. 'Still, I was rather hoping for a sausage or two. I had forgotten the little matter of Bartlemy Fair at this time of year. The neighbours have been rather noisy, but then I started having fun, giving them all a little shake up there. A few extra thrills for their money!'

'What was you getting away from?' Stick tried asking, but she was still talking. He couldn't get a word in edgeways.

'I haven't enjoyed myself so much since I burned the city to a crisp in the Great Fire!' Another giggle. 'A fine bit of mischief, that! You should have seen them scurrying around with their dear little buckets!' But then she turned sulky. 'The fools blamed it on a burned pudding! Or a Frenchman. I don't know which was more insulting!'

Until then, Stick wouldn't have thought it was possible for a snout to pout. He could see it was going to be difficult to keep this beast to the point. But he needed to know what – or who – she'd been running away from. What in tarnation could have put the wind up a dragon like this?

'So you got stuck?' he suggested. 'But where did you

come from? And what was you trying to get away from?'

'Why, from that man, of course.' It *was* fear, he could see it now.

The dragon's snout sniffed at Stick. Her eyes had narrowed to slits of suspicion. But he had no way of expecting what came next.

'You know that man, don't you?' she whispered, accusingly.

She sniffed him again, and her nostrils wrinkled.

'You smell like him.'

If it was possible for a gutterling to get whiter, Stick was so white now you could have seen right through him. 'I don't . . . I ain't like him!'

Those reptilian eyes, pupils narrowed, were fixed on him now. 'So you *do* know him,' she insisted.

Her hot, foul breath was almost suffocating him, she was so close. 'Did he send you down here?' Her teeth were bared and bristling.

'Or are *you* running away from him too?'

CHAPTER 7

The accusing silence between Stick and the dragon was broken by a blowing of whistles and stamping of boots above their heads. The latest upheaval she'd caused to Bartlemy Fair had clearly been the final straw. The police were on the move.

'Strewth! Now you've been and gone and done it!' Stick scolded her. 'The crushers will come fossicking arter us in no time!'

But truth be told, he was glad to change the subject. He didn't want to answer any more questions about that man or how he knew him. And he didn't want to think about why the dragon had said that he and the man smelled the same.

Stick guessed the flummergasted stall-holders had finally forced the forces of law and order out of the alehouse to investigate what was disturbing the peace of Bartlemy Fair. It was only a matter of time before they climbed down there and discovered the dragon's lair. And Stick.

Stick knew that gutterlings like him were sent to prison for nothing or less. 'When in doubt, hang them!' was the motto of the magistrates who sat in judgement at Newgate. 'That'll keep them from picking the pockets of their betters.'

And if hanging was the going rate for being caught in possession of someone else's hankersniff, they would surely string him up twice over for being in possession of a dragon. Especially if she 'fessed up to causing the Fire of London. Even if it was a very long time ago.

'We needs to skedaddle, sharpish!' Stick hissed.

From the look in her bottomless eyes, the dragon was as frightened as he was. 'Which part of "stuck" have you failed to grasp, cabbage-for-brains?' she snapped. 'I can't move, you numbskull!'

Stick briefly considered abandoning her. Why should he saddle himself with saving a creature the size of a juggernaut, particularly one that couldn't keep a civil tongue in her head?

'I could just leave you here, you know,' he snapped back. 'Manners work both ways, missus!'

70

'If you try that, I shall eat you,' came the sharp reply, and the tongue flickered out again and slithered over his bare toes. 'You're far too big to count as a child!'

Stick leaped back like a scalded cat, but there wasn't far he could go, and the shouts were getting louder overhead. It sounded like the crushers had found the same crack in the earth that he had.

'Keep your hair on! Which bit of you is stuck?'

The tongue disappeared again. None of this made Stick feel like he could trust her, but there was no escape, with her massive bulk blocking the tunnel.

'My head.' It was more of a groan now. 'My poor head.' This was followed by what could only be described as a whimper. 'Be a good boy and pop up there and take a look. It does hurt so.'

'Plague take you!' swore Stick, below his breath. One minute she was theatening to snaffle him for lunch, the next she was putting the wheedle on him. 'I never knows where I am with this old buzzard!'

He took another look at the steep cliff of the dragon's face. Scaling it couldn't be much more difficult than climbing up a drainpipe and he'd done that oftentimes when he and the tumblers had been starvacious enough to do a bit of house-cracking. He'd need to have all his buttons about him, to keep from sticking his foot in her eye though. If he did that, he reckoned she'd swallow him whole in a fit of temper.

'If you promise to keep your teeth to yourself, I'll pop up and see if I can get you unstuck. Is it a deal?'

Stick reckoned the brief snort of reply that followed was the closest he was going to get to a promise. He put a cautious hand on top of the hot, flaring nostril next to him, and hoisted himself up, trying to avoid his feet dangling for too long anywhere near her mouth. *Reckon as putting my toes in her chatter-box is just asking for trouble*, he thought.

As he climbed up on to her snout, he could hear the voices of the crushers above him more clearly. He could also hear the clanking of gin bottles as they took a swig of Dutch courage, before they risked sticking their heads down that crack in the ground.

'Cor blimey! It stinks worse than a haddock's armpit!'

'What in all tarnation has died down there?'

Balanced on the snout, Stick felt a rumble. The dragon was stoking up her embers, ready to torch her new visitors.

'Stop it!' he hissed. 'No scorching! We'll never get away if you cause a rumpus!'

12

'God's whiskers!' The rumbling subsided. Her eyes crossed as she tried to focus on him. 'Very well! Stop dithering and get on with it then, jobberknoll! We clearly do not have all day!'

Stick began to clamber up the thick scales between her eyes, using the crusty boils and warts that covered her skin for footholds. 'Poor old carbuncle-face,' he whispered, not too loud, on account of not wanting to cause offence.

At last he reached the top of her head, and whistled softly. 'No wonder you is so cantankerous.'

The dragon's head was crested with spikes that must once have stood upright, as proud as a royal crown, but were now battered and bleeding where they had been crushed against the roof of the tunnel. Every time she had tried to turn around and get out, the wounds must have ripped open again, and her dark, leathery skin was stained with fresh blood and crusted with weeping scabs.

'Cor blimey, missus – you ain't half done yourself a mischief up here.'

'It really is rather painful. Ouch! You clumsy clod-pate!'

Stick was trying to be gentle as his fingers felt around the spikes, but he couldn't think of any way of freeing her that wasn't going to hurt. And make her very, very cross, which didn't seem advisable.

But he had to be quick. From up here, he could hear the crushers drunkenly arguing the toss over who was coming down first. Someone had gone to get a ladder and it was only a matter of time before he and his new acquaintance were going to be arrested. If you could arrest a dragon.

But it ain't going to end well whatever, if we hangs about down here, he thought.

Then his probing fingers found a solution. 'Can you hear me, ma'am?' he asked. He was trying to be polite.

She nodded and let out a loud groan as her wound scraped against the roof. 'God's bodikins! You hurt me, you booberkin!'

'Did you hear that?' came a shout from up above. 'Whatever's down there, it ain't human!'

'I ain't going down there . . .'

There was a clatter, which sounded like the crushers chucking the ladder away. A change of plan. 'Let's load up the muskets, then we can just blow it to kingdom come, whatever it is!'

So now I is going to get shot before I even gets to be hanged! thought Stick gloomily. He was trying to stay calm.

'Listen, ma'am – and try not to nod your noggin again. There's a lump of rock sticking out up here. That's what you has got your bonce stuck on.'

74

'Bonce? Noggin? How dare you!'

Touchy, this dragon. I needs to butter up the old queen, he thought. This wasn't the time to let her take umbrage.

'Your . . . your . . . thingummyjig . . . what looks like a crown . . . like a royal crown . . .'

'Ah, yes, my *corona*! My crowning glory! How it glinted, gold, in the sunlight, as I flew—'

'Yes, ma'am,' interrupted Stick. 'It's stuck. But if you budge your thingummy front-wise . . .' Stick gave the great head a push, gentle as he could. There was a groan of protest, but the spikes shifted.

'And then budge your thingummy side-wise . . .' Another shove and another groan, but the spikes were almost free . . .

'And now, can you dip your head down low, and keep it down. That's it, low as you can . . . that's the daisy-does-it!'

The next groan was a groan of relief, and as Stick slid down the dragon's forehead, great tears rolled down beside him and pooled on her snout.

'Now, ma'am,' said Stick, dancing round to keep his feet dry from the woefuls. 'Whatever you do, you mustn't lift up your thingummybob . . .'

'Corona!' she snapped, almost dislodging him.

75

'Corona then – any road, you mustn't lift it up, or you'll get stuck again like a monkey with its paws in a jar of molasses. And don't you go nodding again, neither!' he added quickly.

He took a deep breath. 'Now, I reckon as you're going to have to go out backwards, 'cos there ain't room for you to turn around. So I is going to slip past your belly, down the tunnel, quick as I can . . .'

'You won't leave me?' She was quite pitiful now.

'No, ma'am, I won't leave you,' he promised. Whether he liked it or not, they were in this together. At least until they had got away from the crushers.

'When I get back there, I is going to get hold of your tail. I presume as you have a tail back there? – NO NODDING! – and I will give it a good tug.

'I is going to help you walk backwards all the way down the tunnel, 'til we get away from these pesky crushers, before they shoots us both to kingdom come with them blasted muskets. And when we get safe, you can tell me all about this cove what you was running away from.'

CHAPTER 8

A couple of hours earlier, back on Pickled Herring Stairs, a raggle-taggle army of gutterlings was setting off on their quest to find Squinty and the other snabbled street-children.

'Stick's got all his buttons on,' reckoned Tree. 'He'll have a plan of his own . . .'

'. . . but Squinty's just a totty-headed little tyke, and he needs us,' finished Cess.

Although if the sisters had known that Stick was closeted under Bartlemy Fair with a dragon the size of the number 10 omnibus they might have been more worried.

So Tree and Cess had come up with a plan. It involved leaving London and going out to the country, wherever that was, which seemed like a risky proposition. But with Fly long gone and Stick missing, the other gutterlings had grudgingly accepted their leadership.

'Any road,' Tree pointed out, 'London stinks to high heaven, and we is all being roasted alive.'

'And it's so blooming hot there's no crossings to sweep and no pockets to pick, what with all the toffs clearing off out of town,' Bandy agreed.

'On top of which,' finished Cess, 'it's the last day of Bartlemy Fair, so there'll be no more drunks to diddle out of their dibs arter today.'

Tom, the horse-yob, who they were now calling Turnip, was allowed to tag along on the grounds that he was the only one who'd ever set foot outside the city gates. He was also the only one who actually had a clue where they were going, but Tree and Cess were determined they weren't going to allow that fact to make him too uppity and above himself.

'Which way then, Turnip-top?' asked Cess.

'North.' He glowered at her from under a pair of fiery ginger brows. 'And me name's Tom.'

'Hark at mister lardy-dardy!' Cess made a face and shrugged at Tree, because how was anybody supposed to know which way north was? Tom shrugged and jerked his thumb instead, which was how it normally worked.

The sisters took the lead, in the direction Stick had taken the night before, past St Paul's and through the heart of the city. The streets on the way to Smithfield were strewn with fair-goers, fuddled and comfoozled by three days of gin and jollification. The churchyards were heaped with people having a little lie-down on the gravestones before heading for home.

'Look at them all, soused as pickled herrings!' sniffed Cess. 'Never seen so many tossicated in one day.'

'It's this blamed heat, gone straight to their daffy heads.' Tree pounced on a meat pie hanging out of the mouth of a man who'd fallen asleep, dribbling, before he'd got round to eating it. She wiped the dribble off and shared the pie out between them all. 'Nobbut one bite each, mind.'

'I ain't half sharp-set,' whined Bandy. 'What we going to do for prog? Is there anything to eat in the country?'

''Course there is,' replied Tom. 'There's apples and pears and plums and all sorts of stuff – you can just help yourself. And if you want a drink you can nip over a fence and borrow some milk off a cow.'

The rest of them stared at him, and somebody snorted because everyone knew that apples came in baskets and milk was made in churns.

'I'll lay there's honey hanging off the trees, and all!' scoffed Bandy.

Tom opened his mouth, then closed it again, because nobody was going to believe him about bees.

Tree turned her back on him. 'Best be on the lookout for vittles and any fall-downs going cheap round Bartlemy Fair.'

Cess joined her. 'We'll stop awhile on the way through Smithfield and see what we can prig for later.'

All the gutterlings knew how to scavenge a living in the city, even if most of them went to sleep hungry most nights, but the country would be a different kettle of fish entirely. Nobody knew what to expect. So when they got to Smithfield they began busily thieving their way around the stalls, filling up Tiddy Doll's basket with prog. It was just about full when Bartlemy Fair was brought to another shuddering standstill.

The earth gave a lurch and the cobbles rattled under their feet and the stalls went crashing to the ground.

'It's just like Stick said,' whispered Cess. 'Same as what happened yesterday!' Tiddy Doll clutched hold of her hand.

'Blimey! Here we go again!' came the grumbles from the stall-holders. All this ruckus was bad for business.

'Might as well shut up shop, if Old Scratch down there keeps this up!'

''Tain't right . . . what's the crushers doing about it?'

80

There was a kerfuffle from the direction of one of the alehouses, and then the heavy tread of boots and blowing of whistles. At last the police were being forced to take notice and find out what was disturbing the peace of the fair.

'Here, look – over here!' One of the crushers had found the crack in the ground.

The gutterlings made the most of the diversion and the distracted crowd to fill their baskets with unguarded vittles, unaware that below their feet Stick was struggling to free the head of a large dragon.

BANG!

There was a rattle of musket-fire.

A stink of sulphur and a blast of scorching air rose from below.

BANG!

More musket-fire. A ripple of excitement shivered through the crowd. This beat the normal entertainment at Bartlemy Fair into a cocked hat.

'Them crushers, didn't think they had it in them!'

'They'll sort it . . .'

But then from below came a shriek of agony and a deep groan. The crowd fell silent, then the uneasy murmurs started.

''Tis Old Nick himself, down there!'

'What the blazes?'

'I knew them crushers would make a mux of it!'

'Better off sending for the priests from St Paul's . . .'

The shriek sounded like souls being tortured to Tree and Cess, who had been weaned by the nuns on stories of purgatory.

'I told you so,' said Tree. 'I said all along, didn't I? Something ain't right.'

This latest ruckus was the last straw for Bartlemy Fair, after three days of comflobstigation and confusion.

'Stuff this for a game of soldiers, I'm off!'

'I ain't hanging around for Old Scratch to drag me downstairs!'

Soon there was a rush of indignant fair-goers streaming away from Smithfied, and the street-sellers gave up and started packing up their battered stalls.

''Tain't right!'

''Tain't normal!'

If there had been any doubts amongst the gutterlings about getting out of the city, they were gone now.

'We needs to scarper,' Tree said firmly, and she and Cess gathered their little troupe around them and set off for the road out to the country, as fast as they could go.

CHAPTER 9

Underground, Stick had still been trying to get the dragon moving when the crushers first opened fire.

BANG!

Sparks flew from the ground as a musket ball narrowly missed the dragon's sprawling belly.

It's like shooting bloaters in a barrel, thought Stick. *Sooner or later me or the old scorcher is going to snuff it – or both of us will – if we don't get a shift on.*

'Time to go, ma'am,' he urged her. 'Remember – you need to keep your temper – and no scorching, or you'll give the game away!'

BANG!

More sparks and puffs of dust, as another musket shot just missed one of the dragon's great taloned feet.

A whimper from the Werme. *All mouth and no trousers, this one*, thought Stick. *Not so highty-tighty now!* But he was having a hard job fighting down the pity. *Don't forget she tried to snaffle you, nobbut five minutes ago*, he reminded himself.

Cobbles began to rain down on them. He reckoned the crushers must have fetched a pickaxe along with the muskets, to open up the crack in the ground.

Stick felt his way quickly along the dragon's belly. Beneath his street-roughened hands her undercarriage felt soft and smooth as a toff's kid gloves. There was enough dim light from above to see that her skin here was the palest greenish-blue, and speckled and dappled like the eggs of a song thrush in spring. Under here, without her armour, she seemed vulnerable for the first time. He knew, without being told, that this was where a dragon-slayer would plunge his lance to make his fatal thrust.

BANG! BANG!

Another couple of musket shots whistled past. A stifled yelp came from the Werme.

'Great snakes! Do something, dunderhead! This is no way for a Werme to meet her Maker!'

Stick reckoned it would take those bone-headed crushers a bit of time to get used to firing the muskets, especially if they were as tossicated as they normally were come the last day of Bartlemy Fair. And they couldn't see what they were aiming at. But it wouldn't be long before the Werme would take a musket ball in the belly and that would make her very, very angry.

And then, dabs to dumplings, I'll end up squashed flat as a flounder, Stick thought.

He slapped the Werme's flank. 'Breathe in, ma'am, and let me squeeze past!'

She was as biddable as a newborn lamb now, and her belly tightened to reveal a set of ribs that wouldn't have looked out of place on the keel of a small ship. As he crept into the narrow gap between dragon and wall, he yelled up, 'I'll give your tail a good tug when I get there! Remember – no nodding, and don't go lifting your bonce or you'll be stuck like a lamprey in an elephant's lughole.' He added quickly, 'And don't breathe out 'til I tug your tail!'

He wondered how long a dragon could hold its breath. Especially when it was under musket-fire.

Lawks! Can't see my hand in front of my face, back here. How big is this beast? The further he went, the darker it got, and Stick was trying hard to forget how much he hated being stuck in the dark, under the ground.

As he squeezed through the cramped space, he tried to think about Fly to take his mind off things. Fly, the sweepling, who'd spent her life wriggling up and down chimbleys narrower than this. Oftentimes she'd told them how she'd had to buff it when her togs got caught on a rough brick. He could hear her now, making all the gutterlings laugh of an evening, telling as how she'd once tumbled out of the fireplace in the middle of a toff's tea-party, wearing nothing but her Adam and Eve's.

Truth be told, he still missed Fly so much it was like she'd left a hole in his heart, even though she'd been gone for months. Usually thinking about Fly made Stick grin, but he wasn't grinning now. If he'd been able to admit it to himself, he would have said he was lonely.

The dragon really didn't count as much of a companion – especially since she still seemed liable to think of him as dinner. In fact, this whole caboodle wasn't much of a lark without Spud and Sparrow. And then he remembered all over again – they could be lying dead somewhere down this tunnel.

I hopes I don't step on them, if they've snuffed it down this festering glory-hole.

In the end, it wasn't the remains of the tumblers he stepped on, but a pile of fresh dragon dung, which smelled every bit as bad as he might have expected. Fear seemed to have loosened her bowels.

But look on the bright side, he thought, trying to ignore the soft squelching between his bare toes. *If a dragon's built anything like a donkey, at least it means I've reached her backside.*

There was more space and it was easier to move now. 'You can breathe out, ma'am,' he yelled up, and there was a great sagging of the belly behind, so she must have heard him.

He felt his way along, beside the long tail. It was spiked, just like the Werme's head, and each spike was smaller than the one before, until at last he reached the end where the spikes were no bigger than his hand.

Just hope them crushers don't hit her before we gets clear — reckon as they're too bosky to shoot straight. He couldn't hear much of what was going on at the front because the dragon's body was muffling the sound, but from the regular jumps and shivers that kept running down her spine, he reckoned the dragon was still under musket-fire.

'Here goes, then!' Stick tugged hard on her tail. A shudder of offended pride rippled down her spine, but there was no more than a moment of hesitation before the great bulk of a dragon pulled her body up into a low crouch and strained to heave herself backwards.

He could see there was no dignity in all this for a Werme, being pulled by the tail like an eel out of a plug hole. He was glad he couldn't hear much from the front, because she was probably cursing like a costermonger. She did let off some ripe farts, which didn't make his position at her rear end exactly a bed of roses. *Strewth! That Punch and Judy show ain't half disagreed with Milady Gobble-guts!*

He could hear the musket shots coming quicker now, as the crushers got the hang of reloading. And even though the dragon seemed to have shifted a little, she was still stuck, and when all was said and done, she was simply too big for his tugging to make much difference.

'Bust me!' Stick groaned in frustration. How was he ever going to get her out? *She's rammed in here like a cork in a brandy bottle!*

Stick went right to the end of the tail and, grasping it with two hands, gave it an almighty heave. Again and again he pulled, but still nothing moved, and the crack of musket-fire kept coming. He could feel the dragon shaking in terror. It seemed like an age that he had been struggling and tugging, and he was starting to despair.

'Breathe in, ma'am, and remember, keep your head down!' he yelled. 'Now, one more try!' He grabbed her tail once more and pulled with all his strength, bracing his heels against the floor of the tunnel.

At last, something shifted. Stick went flying as the Werme took her first step backwards, and a ripple of excitement shivered through her tail. She was free!

It was slow progress at first. Stick could hear her soft belly scraping against the tunnel and rubbing her skin raw.

Poor old crumpet-face, he thought as he broke into a run down the tunnel, praying she wouldn't trample him into fish-porridge as she gathered pace after him. *She must have wanted that sausage really bad.* Or else been really scared of the man she was running away from.

Who is that cove that could scare the living daylights out of a dragon? But in his heart he already knew. If he followed this tunnel to its end he was going to have to face what he'd run away from, all those years ago. And truth be told, he was every bit as scared as the Werme.

But then, just as he was thinking they were safe, and that she must be out of shot for the sozzled crushers and their muskets, a great shriek and shudder of pain came from the front. 'Croopus!' Stick muttered. 'That's enough to wake King Billy in his feather-bed, up at Buckanory Palace!'

He started to run, guiding her along as fast as he could in

the darkness. He was stumbling over dried dragon dung and other objects that rattled against his feet and sounded suspiciously like bones, so maybe it was good he couldn't see. The dragon backed up behind him, but with every step came the terrible keening of a beast in pain.

'Keep up, old queen,' he called back. 'I swear I'll get you out of here, even if I swings on the gallows for it!'

CHAPTER 10

'Watch where you're putting them plates o' meat!' Stick yelled. He had just dodged being skewered by the sharp horn on the back of her heel.

It wasn't a comfortable thing to be running backwards and in constant danger of being crushed into bloater-paste. Stick was almost deafened by the unholy racket she was making, and they'd been running for almost a mile by his reckoning.

'Stow that row!' he shouted at the dragon, who was still blundering back-to-front behind him. 'If you don't shut your palaver the crushers will follow us down here! We needs them to think you've stuck your spoon in the wall!'

The wailing subsided into a hiccup and a whimper, and then a puzzled murmur. 'Spoon?'

'Kicked the bucket, hopped the twig, ma'am – what I means is, we needs them to think you're dead. The last thing them dunderheads want to do is to have to come down here. They're already scared out of the few wits they was born with – so if we keep mum, mebbe they'll leave us in peace.'

'But my paw hurts so.'

Stick would hardly have described what this beast had on the end of her legs as 'paws', but it made her sound so pitiful he turned back and patted her flank. He could feel with every step she was limping and flinching with pain.

'Look, ma'am, I reckon we can slow down now. And if we go on a bit further and the tunnel gets a bit wider, mebbe we can stop and you can turn round and I'll take a look at your . . . your paw.'

'There's a place . . . ahead. There's . . . water . . .'

She was puffing and struggling to get her breath, and Stick wondered, not for the first time, how old this creature was. *Too old to be racketing about down here with a bunch of clod-pates taking pot-shots at her with their muskets, that's for certain*, he thought.

'Poor old crumpet-face.' He stroked her soft belly as she slowed to a brisk, wincing waddle.

'Crumpets?' She sounded as eager as she had when he'd mentioned sausages. 'I LOVE crumpets. Plenty of fresh butter, so it oozes into those dear little holes, you know?'

'I know,' said Stick, who was partial to a crumpet himself, but was wondering how the blazes a dragon could ever have partaken of one – with or without fresh butter. 'Me too.'

They both fell silent, and Stick assumed that like him, old guzzle-guts was thinking about crumpets. It was a long time since he'd had those saveloys, and fear is a great sharpener of the appetite. He wasn't rightly sure when the dragon had last eaten, and he wasn't inclined to credit anything she said on that score anyways. He just hoped the Punch and Judy man had filled enough of a hole to keep her from noshing on him.

Now she was quiet, he strained his ears to listen for signs that the crushers might be coming after them. They'd put a good distance between them and her lair under Smithfield, and it all sounded quiet back there.

They ain't going to come fossicking about down here, if they can help it, he thought. *They'll tell the magistrates that whatever unnatural beast was causing all that shemozzle, they has blown out its lights, and there's nowt left for anyone to get into a pother about.*

What he could hear though, now the dragon had shut her mollocking, was the unmistakable sound of rushing water. He squinted into the darkness ahead – he could see light slanting down into the tunnel. He stumbled quickly towards it, giving the dragon's tail an encouraging tug.

'There's room to turn round now, ma'am,' he called out.

Ahead of him the tunnel widened into a large cavern. The walls were dripping wet, and through it tumbled a torrent of crystal-clear water that sparkled in the light from a shaft above.

'What the mischief? If it ain't a river – a river underground!'

Forgetting about his companion, Stick waded into the shallows, feeling the soft sand of the riverbed soothing his heat-blistered feet.

'Croopus, I ain't half parched!' He squatted down quickly and sank his face into the cool water.

A moment later he found himself flat on his backside in the shallows as an immense craggy head plunged in beside him, knocking him sideways. Bubbles of what was unmistakably laughter burst to the surface from her nostrils.

'What the blazes did you do that for?' gasped Stick. 'Me sit-upons is soaked through!'

'Do you good to have a wash, young man!' she said, with what could only be described as a schoolgirl giggle. 'Besides, the water here is very clean.

'This is London's lost river. Everyone has forgotten it is here but me, which is why it is the only river your disgusting species hasn't turned into a sewer. It runs down to the Thames, under the city.'

Now that Stick's body had got over the shock of the unaccustomed feel of clean water on his skin, he found it wasn't half bad. He gave his legs a trial rub, and watched years of dirt flowing away.

The dragon was slurping the fresh water greedily beside him, steam rising gently where her nostrils met the stream. Without thinking, he reached out and touched her muzzle. It was surprisingly soft.

'We made it, ma'am,' he said. 'We got away.'

CHAPTER 11

For Tree and Cess and their gang of gutterlings, the road north from Smithfield to the country lay through some of the meanest and darkest slums London had to offer.

Even after weeks of stifling heat, the narrow lanes between the rotting tenements ran wet with mud and worse; they were ankle-deep with rubbish and teeming with rats. The tenements were so tall they blocked out the sunlight, and so rickety they had to be propped apart with thick beams to prevent them lurching into each other's arms like long-lost lovers.

The toffs – who never stepped foot in there – called this place the Rookeries, because it was easier to pretend that the cries that came out of there were from wild birds, rather than humans like themselves.

A group of mirksy coves with a hang-gallows look about them were loitering at the end of one of the lanes that led into the dark heart of the place. They were gleering at the gutterlings. It was to keep out of the way of such havey-cavey types that the gutterlings chose to sleep on the streets.

'Best mizzle, my cullies,' Cess said uneasily.

Tree nodded and they quickened their pace as they passed the locals. 'I don't like the look of that shravey lot.'

A wizened old crone was sitting next to the open sewer that trickled down into the street, taking the air. In spite of the heat she was wrapped in layers of shabby shawls, like she couldn't trust anyone not to steal them if she put them down for a moment. Taking out the short pipe she was smoking, she aimed a long tobacco-stained jet of spittle at the gutterlings as they scurried past. It was nothing personal – she'd have done the same for any stranger.

'Filthy old trout,' Tree commented, but not loud enough to risk giving offence.

It was a relief to leave the slums behind them – it was not a place where anyone would want to dawdle as the dusk drew in. The road widened into an empty no man's land of scrubby earth, which was being torn up on either side of the road to make way for new streets. Rows and rows of mean little houses, two-up, two-down, were being thrown

97

together as fast as mud could be torn out of the earth and baked into bricks.

Tom looked about him and whistled. 'So this be why they is in such a hurry-scurry for bricks,' he said. 'We bakes bricks in my village,' he told the gutterlings in explanation. He sounded wistful, but there was also a touch of pride.

But nobody was much interested in the Turnip and his tall tales. They were more worried about where they were going to spend the night in this unfamiliar, hostile territory.

'My pa digs out the clay and they bakes it in ovens,' Tom insisted, but more loudly now, determined to be heard. But that just made everyone laugh.

'Don't be daffy! You bakes bread in ovens, not bricks!' sniffed Cess.

'I suppose your ma knits the roofs out of grass!' Bandy jeered.

'Well, and what if she do?' Tom shouted, squaring up to Bandy and dancing on his toes in front of him like a prize boxer, offering his fists to Bandy's face. 'I'll give you a larruping you'll never forget, you lummox, if you poke fun at my ma!'

'Stow your jabber, Bandy,' snapped Tree, but Bandy was already backing away. Country-fed Tom was a lot sturdier than the rickety-legged crossing-sweep, who was as skinny as a streak of mud.

They walked on in silence.

'My ears is empty,' observed Tiddy Doll.

Everyone listened. 'She's right,' said Bandy. 'There ain't nothing to put in them.'

The gutterlings were missing the cries from the late pie-men and the shouts from street brawls and the songs of ballad-singers. It was too quiet. And it was making everyone feel even more uneasy about what lay ahead.

But then . . . 'What's that?' Cess demanded. They were all on alert for every sound.

Tom peered back into the thick yellow heat-smog of the city behind them. 'There's a carriage coming!' he shouted.

There was a rattle of wheels, a thundering of hooves, and it was upon them.

The carriage was all black and it was pulled by four huge black horses that had been whipped so hard they were wild-eyed and frothing white at the mouth. The coachman cursed and pulled hard on the reins as the horses whinnied and reared at the sight of the gutterlings in their path.

'Get out of the road!' screamed Tree, shoving the others aside. Just in the nick of time they scattered into the ditches on each side of the lane.

99

'Tiddy!' screamed Cess.

The flower-girl, laden with her basket, was slower to run away, and the hooves of the leading horses reared high over her head as the carriage careered to a halt. A great hoof crashed to the ground as Cess pulled her to safety, just a moment from it crushing her skull.

'Blimey, Tiddy!' Cess hugged her. 'That was tarnal close!'

The window of the carriage slammed open and a man leered out. 'Drive on!' he yelled up to the coachman. 'Why have you stopped?' His face was as red as beetroot and he had a pickaxe for a nose.

A hatchet-faced woman poked her head out above his. Her hollow cheeks were the same bilious shade as the man's, and she had far too much nose for her face. She was as skinny as he was wide, but apart from that, it was no flattery to say they were as alike as peas in a pod.

'Did you not hear his Lordship?' she shrieked at the coachman. 'What are you waiting for, you fool?'

'Beg pardon, ma'am!' The coachman whipped the horses on again, and in a moment the carriage was gone, its wheels churning up a cloud of choking dust.

'Cor, he must be off his chump, driving like that – like the hounds of Hell is arter him!' whistled Bandy.

'Or the hounds of Hell is in there with him,' replied Tree grimly. 'Did you cop a look at them faces, gleering out at us?'

'It were that woman what's been snabbling the childers.' Cess was pale and grim-faced as she dusted Tiddy Doll's skirt down and checked her over for bruises.

Tree swore. 'Drabbit it! And I'll lay that's the dicey cove what made Stick jumpy as a basketful of weasels in there with her!'

'And did you see who else was in there?' Bandy had ended up in the opposite ditch when they scattered. 'It were Squinty, I swear. I saw him, staring out the windy. He looked scared out of his wits!'

'What few wits he's got!' muttered Tree darkly, who still hadn't forgiven Squinty for being fool enough to fall for the plum duff. 'That lad's about as cunning as a dead pig.'

'Any road,' Tom stood in front of them with his hands on his hips. 'I were right.'

They all stared at him.

'What do you mean, you were right, Turnip-top?' snapped Cess. She didn't like the way he was looking so pleased with himself.

'That's the self-same carriage – and that's the self-same cove – what I saw with Stick, all them years ago, all togged

101

up like a swell. So you had better shut up and stop calling me Turnip, 'cos I'm the only one who knows where we're going. And if you wants somewhere warm and safe to kip for the night, you'd better hold your hush and follow me.'

CHAPTER 12

Stick and the dragon sat companionably in the shallows of the cool river. The dragon was amusing herself by blowing bubbles from her nostrils, and watching, cross-eyed, as the water turned into steam.

The old fossil's easily amused, he thought. *But mebbe she's just happy not to be stuck . . .*

As for him, he was simply enjoying the fact that he wasn't too hot for the first time in a long time. But at last he said, 'Let's have a gander at that foot of yours.'

She almost overbalanced as she tried to plonk her injured foot on to his knee. It would have been curtains for Stick if she'd toppled over on him.

'Whoa, hold up, ma'am, mebbe put it down there, next to me.'

He stood up to take a look. His kecks were still dripping, but it was a refreshing change from being roasted. Sharing a tunnel with a dragon was like being banged up in a baker's oven.

'Boil me!' he whistled. 'No wonder you've got the dolefuls! They ain't half made a mess of that!'

The musket shot had blown the flesh away around one of her talons, leaving a ragged hole clean through the dragon's foot. The skin around it was already looking swollen. Stick knew he would have to work fast if he was going to be able to stop it festering. He'd known too many gutterlings carried off by fever from sores that had gone bad.

'First thing, I needs to give your poor trotter a good wash.'

The river ran red as the dragon gingerly lowered her foot into the stream. She gave a hot snort of pain that singed the hairs on the back of Stick's neck as he bent over to clean the wound.

The gutterlings had learned to come to him with the sores and scrapes and fevers that went with life on the streets. Not that he could always do much. Oftentimes it was too late, and no amount of physicking could help. Stick never let himself think about the hands that he had watched doing stuff like this, nor where he got his skills with healing.

When the wound was clean, Stick stepped back and looked the beast, as best he could, straight in the eye.

'Listen, ma'am, I needs to do something that is really going to hurt. But if I don't do it, you could get real sick. So I needs you to promise me two things. One – that you will hold your hush and not make a hullabaloo. And two – that you won't come over so curmudgeonly that you forget yerself and gobble me up.'

The dragon looked shifty and gave a non-committal grunt.

'I can't rightly hear you,' Stick persisted, cupping his hand round his ear.

The dragon looked at her blood, which was still staining the water scarlet. 'God's fish! Oh, very well. But be quick.'

It was clearly the closest he was going to get to a promise.

From one pocket Stick took out his pipe and put it in his mouth to steady his nerves. From the other he took out the ivory-backed penknife that was his pride and joy, picked from a toff's pocket up West. Spud had wanted to flog it, straight off, but Stick hadn't been able to bear parting with it.

'Here, ma'am, there's a log washed up over there – why don't you bite down on that?' It seemed a good idea for her to have something in her chatter-box that wasn't him.

Stick waded back over to the injured foot. He flicked open the penknife and tested the sharp blade lightly on his finger. 'Here goes . . .' He took a deep breath, clenching the pipe between his teeth, and cut deep into her ragged flesh.

A shudder of pain went through the beast, but, fair dues, she didn't let out a peep or pull her foot away. Or bite his head off.

Stick reached up and patted her flank. 'That's a brave old queen,' he soothed her. 'Just a bit more now.'

Again and again he sliced into the wound, probing it with the tip of the knife to clean out the musket shot and the dirt from the tunnel. At last he stood back, satisfied, and looked up at the dragon.

'There. Clean as a whistle.'

The last thing Stick did was to wash out what was left of his threadbare shirt and hold it up to the dragon's nostrils.

'Here, missus, can you blow a bit of hot on that – not too much, mind, or you'll burn it to a frazzle.'

She gave an obedient snort, and in moments the shirt was dry. Stick wrapped it round her wound and tied it like a bandage.

'There, that's all rug for now. But what I could really do with is some herbs to make a poultice . . .'

He glanced up at the dragon. She was staring at her bandaged foot, and he could have sworn her eyes were brimming with the woefuls once more.

'Cheer up, ma'am – no call to be in such a colly-molly.'

'Why are you being so kind?' she snapped. A flash of suspicion. 'It's not what I've come to expect from humans.'

Stick shrugged. 'Don't rightly know, ma'am.' He really wasn't too sure himself, truth be told. 'But one good turn deserves another – now I has sorted your trotter out – why don't you tell me a bit more about that man?'

The dragon gave a fratchety snort. From the look that crossed her scaly face, Stick reckoned the ungrateful old bag would still rather eat him than have to tell him what he wanted to know.

Her jaws gaped open and Stick sprang quickly backwards into the shallows of the river, ready to scarper. But the gape just ended in a lazy yawn. 'Very well, boy. First I need a nap, though, after all that to-do.' She sank down and stretched her great length out along the river bank. In moments she was snoring.

Stick watched her for a while. He was thinking. High above his head the shaft of daylight was fading to dusk.

108

Now would be the time to do a bunk, to leave her there and carry on down the tunnel, to carry on his search for Spud and Sparrow. He still had no idea what had happened to them.

He was trying not to think about how much he hated being shut up underground. It was taking all his strength to fight down the memories that being down here in the dark was bringing back.

But in the end, he shrugged again, and paddled back to the dragon. *His* dragon, he caught himself thinking.

She had rolled on to her side, like a dog begging for a tummy tickle. It must feel so good to her, not to be wedged upright like a herring in a barrel. How vulnerable she looked, with that soft thrush-egg belly rising and falling in time to her snores.

He hesitated. The air was chillier now, without his shirt. He crept over and lowered himself to lean his back against her smooth skin. It wasn't warm, but there was comfort in it. At least she was another living thing, however unreliable.

'Who'd credit it, me snoozled up with a dragon!' Stick said, softly. 'Reckon I ain't never slept so snug.'

Before Stick closed his eyes, he glanced up at the shaft above his head. There was an ominous glow to the night sky that puzzled him.

109

But by the time a blood-red moon rose to cast its baleful light down on to the pair of them, Stick was fast asleep.

And he had long ago forgotten being told what it meant when the moon turned red.

CHAPTER 13

After the near miss with the carriage, Tree and Cess had decided they had to rely on Tom to find them somewhere safe to sleep for the night. They didn't like handing over the lead to anyone, especially to a stranger and a country joskin at that, but they'd looked at each other and at everyone else, and nodded in silent agreement.

So the gaggle of gutterlings had followed Tom into the gathering darkness, huddling close for comfort.

The air was thick with late summer smells, sweet and musty and ripe, and full of sounds none of the gutterlings had ever heard before – hoots and grunts and sudden howls, and the pattering of feet belonging to creatures they couldn't see and didn't want to guess at. The silence in between the noises was even worse. In all their born days, none of the city urchins had ever heard silence like this.

'Blimey, it ain't half quiet,' whispered Bandy.

''Tain't natural,' sniffed Cess.

'But it don't half smell better.' Tiddy Doll lifted her small smiling face to the evening stars and sniffed. 'I wish I could stay in the country for ever.' After weeks of being roasted like chestnuts, the gutterlings were breathing cool, fresh air at last.

It was almost dark, with not a glim of a gaslight to be seen, when Tom stopped and peered through a gap in the hedge.

'Come on,' he called back impatiently, as they hesitated to follow. 'I'll have you tucked up snug in less than a pig's whisper.' He slipped through the gap and disappeared.

Cess shrugged. 'Reckon we ain't got much choice.'

So the band of gutterlings climbed after Tom, to make the close acquaintance of the first field they had ever met.

'Blimey, this stuff don't half tickle!' protested Bandy. The stubble of the newly harvested hay prickled at their bare feet and scratched at their ankles.

'I just trod in something,' whimpered Tiddy Doll. For the first time in her life she was the proud owner of a pair of shoes that she'd found discarded up at Covent Garden. So

112

she was the only one with anything on their feet to get spoiled. She was also the only one with blisters.

'Over here!' Tom's voice came from the middle of the field. As they struggled over to him, the outline of something the size of a hackney carriage loomed out of the dark.

'It's a haystack,' he announced, as proud as if he'd invented haystacks himself. He scrambled up the heap of dry hay, showering bits on to them below, and called down, 'Prime place for a good night's kip!'

They were still looking doubtful, so he lay on his stomach and hung off the edge. 'Here – Tiddy – hold up your dib-dabs, and I'll pull you up!'

Tiddy Doll limped doubtfully over to the haystack and reached her hands up to him. Light as a feather, she fairly flew as he hoisted her to the top.

'Anyone else?'

One by one they scrambled up the haystack, and Tom showed them how to burrow their way in, so they ended up with just their heads sticking out, like so many hat pins in a lady's poke-bonnet. Soon they were all tucked up tight in the fresh-cut hay, which was still warm from the sun and smelled as sweet as new-baked bread.

'Blimey, I is nibblish hungry – where's the nosh?' Bandy demanded, and Tiddy Doll wriggled her arms free

113

to unpack her basket and hand out bits of cold pie and sausage.

'Cor, look at us, scoffing our supper in bed, like a fine set of swells!' Bandy whistled.

'Ain't this naffy?' whispered Tiddy Doll. Her face was tilted up to the darkening sky. 'Looks like blue velvet up there, like I saw on a lady's gown one time, up Covent Garden. She let me touch it, and it were the most beautiful thing I ever saw, 'til now.'

Tiddy stretched her thin arms up towards the stars, and there was a lifetime of longing in her fingers. 'Makes you want to reach up and stroke it.' She sighed. 'I hates the dark, normal-times, 'cos I never knows who's lurking out there.'

'You ain't never come to no harm when you've been with us,' objected Cess.

'No, Cess, you has always looked out for me.' Tiddy stretched over and wrapped her arms round Cess's neck. 'But I can't rightly remember when I had a roosting-ken so safe and snug as this. I loves it here.'

'It's all rug,' Cess admitted, grudgingly.

Tree joined in. 'You've done us proud, Turnip!'

It was the first good word she'd had to say for him. But her praise was stifled when Tom leaned over and stuffed a handful of hay over her head.

114

'Tom, then!' she shrieked. The sound of laughter was strange – it felt like none of them had laughed for a long time.

But Bandy sobered them up. 'We was lucky we didn't get scrobbled by them two on the road back there, along with Squinty.'

'Too many of us, mebbe?' suggested Tiddy Doll.

'Mebbe.'

Silence.

'Them two be wicked clean through and through,' said Tom, suddenly, into the darkness. It sounded like he'd got a chicken bone stuck in his throat. 'The childers in my village, they kept disappearing, and nobody dared say nuffin, because that toff, Sir Jasper, he owns the whole place, and nobody gets no job in the brickworks without his say-so.

'Nobody knows what him and his sister has done with all the kinchen. Then my little sister got snaffled. It were so quiet at home without her, and my ma just wouldn't stop crying.'

Another pause, then he went on. 'Sweet little thing, she is, but bossy with it. I calls her Marm 'cos she's got these orange curls, like marmalade, you know.' Tom swallowed hard. 'I wanted to go and look for her, but my ma said as she couldn't bear it if they got me too. That's why she sent me away.' He stopped for a moment, then added quietly, 'I didn't tell you afore, 'cos I thought you wouldn't come with me.'

Silence.

'We'd have come with you any road, Tom.' Tree's voice was as gruff as his. 'They've snabbled our own, along with yours.'

'And we're going to get them back!' Cess was trying to sound like she believed it.

Silence again, as they all stared out into the darkness and contemplated what lay ahead. But it had been a long day, and one by one they fell asleep. So it was only Tom who saw the full moon rise above the trees.

It was blood red. And it stained the landscape the colour of anger.

'A Blood Moon,' Tom whispered to himself.

He was the only one with the country lore to know that a Blood Moon always brought death in its wake. And he could tell that it was rising over the place towards which they were heading.

The place he called home.

CHAPTER 14

Back under the streets of London, it was still black as pitch when Stick woke up the next morning. He had no idea how far they had run the day before, and what part of the city lay above his head.

It took him a while to work out that the gurgling next to his ear wasn't coming from a blocked sewer, but from the grumbling guts of the beast he'd been using as a pillow. His own guts were grumbling too, but he reckoned the dragon being hungry was more of a worry, no matter how starvacious he was himself.

Won't matter much if my belly's empty, if I ends up filling hers. Leastwise, I wouldn't be hungry no more, he mused. *Wonder how often she needs to nosh, whether she's a three-square-meals-a-day kind of creature, or just likes a big blow-out now and then?* He was still lamentably short of facts when it came to dragons.

Stick got up and stretched, then rubbed at his bare arms. It had grown chilly during the night and although there hadn't been a lot left of his shirt, he'd been fond of it. He crept closer to the dragon's nostrils, and stood warming himself for a while in her breath, wishing it would get light.

He always found it harder to think in the dark. Tentacles of long-buried memories had a way of wrapping themselves around his thoughts when he was alone in the dark.

At last, pink fingers of dawn began to poke holes in the blue blanket of sky above his head. The dragon was still determinedly fast asleep, so Stick went down for a drink. He considered going for another wash but two washes within a matter of hours surely couldn't be good for the constitution, and he cautioned himself against it.

Across the river, the tunnel stretched ahead into the unknown. *Down there must be where she came from*, thought Stick, staring into the darkness and not wanting to think too much about what lay at the end of it.

The early-morning sun was sending a shaft of light down on to the underground river that had carved its way through the rock-bed.

118

Reckon it ain't so wide as normal-times, thought Stick. It looked like the Great Heat had shrunk the river, leaving a narrow bank on each side, although the torrent at the centre still flowed fast down towards the Thames.

Remembering his friend Fly's advice never to be stuck anywhere without knowing the whereabouts of all the exits, Stick glanced back to check that the dragon was still sleeping, and set off down the riverbank to explore.

The life and the smells of the stirring city leaked down through gratings in the street above.

'Get it hot here! Hot pies! Hot and hot!'

'Cawfee! Strong enough to stand yer spoon up!'

It all seemed a long and lonely way off as Stick scrambled and slithered along the wet rock.

Croopus! It wouldn't half give them up there a nasty turn, if they knew what was lurking under their feet.

That thought reminded him of something. *That's what that cove was saying, back at Bartlemy Fair, when Spud and Sparrow got snabbled! What was it?* Then Stick remembered. *'You fools . . . you know not what lies beneath!'* That was it.

Stick was beginning to put it all together. That man, the man he feared above all others – he'd known exactly what was causing such a rumpus at the fair. That's how it all connected up!

119

That's what he was doing there, Stick thought. *He were looking for the dragon. But he mustn't have spotted the crack in the ground . . .*

Stick frowned. *I'll lay the dragon knows what he's up to – somehow I has to wheedle the truth out of her. She has to tell me . . .*

But he was still trying to squash the fear that the man had also snabbled Spud and Sparrow in that big bag of his. Worry was worming at Stick's guts like a two-day hunger.

He was about to turn back, determined to get some answers out of the dragon, when he came to another shaft of light, striped with shadows from iron bars above. This time, the sounds from the surface stopped him dead in his tracks.

The hammering of nails. Shouts and grunts that sounded like workmen heaving something heavy into place. More hammering.

'All ready. Let them in!'

The sound of iron gates shrieking on their hinges. Hundreds of pairs of boots clattering into an echoing cobbled yard. A surge of feverish chatter, bubbling over with excitement.

A gasp and silence. And then the ominous shuffle of just one pair of feet, slow and reluctant on wooden planks.

120

The feet were stumbling as if the person they belonged to was being pushed from behind.

Stick shivered. *'Tis Newgate up there . . .*

He didn't need to see what was happening on the gallows in the prison yard above his head. He'd heard it described by gutterlings who'd joined the queue to watch this early-morning spectacle.

A Newgate hanging. The best antidote for three days of sin and tossification at Bartlemy Fair. It was London's favourite show – cost you no more than getting out of bed early of a morning. And you could even make a shilling or two by laying a bet on whether they'd hang them with their face to the clock or looking down Ludgate Hill.

'Half-past hanging time and time to hang again!' went the old rhyme. If the crowds were lucky they'd get more than one hanging today, depending on the mood of the magistrates and how much fine claret they'd had with their slap-up dinner before delivering their judgement. The beaks decided whether you were transported for life or scragged on the gallows, and good riddance as far as they were concerned.

Stick and the tumblers had never been inside Newgate, but they'd known those who'd ended up swinging from those gallows, and a fair few who'd been left to rot underground in its dark stone cells. Going to watch a

121

hanging was too close for comfort, Stick had always thought. And it was too close for comfort now.

He clapped his hands over his ears and fled, so he didn't hear the final agonised pleas for mercy or the groan from the frenzied crowd. He stumbled back down the riverbank, sickened and still shivering.

'WHERE HAVE YOU BEEN?!'

Gone was the pitiful, whimpering, wretched creature that had lain so still and meek the night before, whilst Stick physicked her foot. This dragon was reared up to half her full height, as high as the cavern roof would allow, and she looked every bit as wicked as the creature he'd seen on the top of the city gate.

'HOW DARE YOU LEAVE ME?!'

She didn't even look the same colour with the morning sun streaming down on her from the shaft above. Her scales were more a kind of mildewed green now rather than dusty yellow. He hadn't even noticed her leathery wings before. The undersides were the palest crimson and though they were still no more than half unfurled, they contained a sense of brooding power.

It was the first time since Stick had made her acquaintance that the dragon hadn't been crawling on her belly. As she glared down on him, no doubt planning to give him a good scorching as a punishment for leaving her, he had to admit she was a formidable sight.

He took a deep breath. Her roar would have been enough to make a lesser lad turn tail and take their chances back down the river, but Stick wasn't one to give up on an adventure that easily. And a bit of flummery had worked last time.

'Cor, ma'am,' he whistled in admiration. 'I see now why you call that thing a crown! Them spikes is sticking up a real treat, and don't it just shine like sovereign gold, up there on the top of your bonce!'

Sure enough, the flames she'd been stoking up to punish him subsided into an interested snort, and the vain old curmudgeon twisted round to catch a look at herself in the reflection from the river.

'Do you really think it looks better?' she inquired anxiously, squinting at her corona from every angle. 'It's been squashed flat in that horrid tunnel for so long, I feared it might not recover.'

'Mebbe if you lets me take a look, ma'am? And then I'll check on your foot arter that.'

She grunted, scorching forgotten for now. This dragon's moods could change in a blink of her scaly eyelids.

She bowed her head obediently so Stick could squint up at the injured spikes.

'I reckon they could do with a good wash, ma'am. If you dunks your noddle – your head, I mean – down into the river, it would do them sore spikes no end of good.' *And mebbe cool down those flames*, he thought to himself, still not convinced she wouldn't turn round any moment and give him a roasting.

'And after that you can tell me the truth about where you come from, like you promised last night,' he added firmly. 'Is it a deal?'

'I suppose so . . .' She took a deep breath and dunked her head into the torrent. There was a huge splash and a great hiss of steam as the heat from her nostrils met the water.

Stick scrambled up and along the arch of her bowed neck to reach the spikes, which were still above the water. Gingerly, and as gently as he could, he washed away the dirt-encrusted scabs and cleaned the wounds where they had been rubbed raw against the roof of the tunnel.

He sat back at last, satisfied, and tapped the dragon on her shoulder. 'You can come up now.'

124

She reared up, and gave a violent shake of her head.

Stick, who had been squatting on her forehead wondering idly why a beast that size had such very small ears, was thrown off into the fast-flowing water in the centre of the river. He hadn't expected her to come up so quickly – and he didn't even have time to think whether that shake had been deliberate.

'Ma'am!' he cried as he went under. 'I can't swim!'

His head surfaced again, but before he had time to gasp 'Help me!' the swift current seized him. He was dragged down and swept rapidly away, towards the outflow to the Thames.

CHAPTER 15

There had been long hours of walking before the gutterlings neared Tom's home village, and the novelty of being able to hop over the fence to filch apples or stuff their faces with free blackberries from the hedgerow was wearing off fast.

They had woken at dawn at the top of the golden haystack in the middle of a field of silver dew, whilst back beneath London, Stick was listening to the sound of the gallows being built at Newgate.

By now the sun was high in the sky and even the wonder of having Tom squirt warm milk into their mouths from the underside of a cow was forgotten. Especially since some cove had turned up and chased them off, brandishing a big stick. 'Thieving little tykes!'

'Turns out the country's just like the city, then, Turnip!' panted Bandy, as they'd skedaddled down the lane.

It was good to be able to breathe again, after weeks of the stifling Great Heat, but by midday the August sun was beating down something fierce.

'Me feet is killing me,' whispered Tiddy Doll to Cess.

'Not surprised, wearing them shummocky trotter-boxes!' replied Cess.

Tiddy Doll looked down at her blistered feet. 'You're right. They is about as much use as a hat on a hen!'

She sighed. It had been giving her a great deal of pleasure, sneaking secret glances at those shoes. But she knew they weren't for the likes of her, so she chucked them over the hedge and walked barefoot, as she usually did.

Tree was watching Tom's face. She and Cess had grudgingly admitted their street wisdom was useless out here and so were letting him lead the way. He'd been setting a fast pace, looking back impatiently and urging them all on, but now he slowed down, peering through the hedgerows into the fields, like he was puzzled about something.

Tree gave Cess a silent nod, and the pair of them drew up close to him. 'Something wrong, ain't it?' Tree kept her voice down so the others couldn't hear.

Tom nodded. 'Look!' He was pale under his freckles, which had decided it might be safe to return now they were back in the country.

He was pointing at a field. The sisters looked. It was a field. And as far as they could see, it looked much the same as all the other fields they walked past. No buildings. No shops. And lots of grass. Only difference was, this grass was a kind of golden colour, and tall, so it was waving about in the breeze.

'What's wrong with it?' puzzled Cess. 'It's just grass, ain't it?'

Tom looked at her. 'It be wheat, you clod-pate!'

The sisters both looked blank.

'Wheat – you know, what flour be made from – what bread be made from . . .'

Still blank.

Tom sighed and went on as if he was explaining to a pair of nick-ninnies. 'The whole village ought to be out here, getting in the harvest – cutting it down while it's ripe. If it rains, it'll all be ruinated – there'll be nowt to eat all winter.' They could hear panic in his voice. 'But there bain't nobody there. Where be they all?'

To the gutterlings – whose vittles mostly fell off the backs of stalls – he might as well have been talking Double

Dutch, but they could see it was something that really mattered to a splodger like Tom.

Tree and Cess squinted into the sun. Tom was right, there wasn't a soul in sight. Just field upon field of wavy yellow stuff. Wheat, according to the Turnip.

'Mebbe they is all sick . . .'

'Or mebbe they just didn't fancy it today . . .'

'Mebbe they wanted a lie-in – it ain't half hot, arter all . . .'

'Or mebbe they is all down the alehouse?'

Tom stared at them like they'd gone clean off their dots, and nothing they came up with seemed to reassure him, so they carried on in silence for another mile.

'Ain't we there yet?' called Bandy, who was lagging behind. 'My belly's crying cupboard.'

Tom nodded. 'It's just over that hill.' He pointed ahead. 'Come on, guzzle-guts! I'll lay Ma will have a big pan of rabbit stew on the go. You can stuff yourselves silly.'

But his grim-set face was telling a different story. He didn't look like he really believed in that rabbit stew.

With a deep breath of faith, Tom turned off the road up a narrow jumble-gut lane that looked like a tunnel. It sloped gently upwards between steep, green banks topped with red-berried hedgerows. The gutterlings trailed up the hill after him, dodging the deep ruts baked hard by weeks of drought.

Nobody was saying much. They'd picked up on Tom's fear.

When they caught up with Tom at the top, he was staring down at a hamlet of white stone cottages, nestled in the shelter of the valley. Glowering over the village was a mansion built from black bricks and choked with ivy. And encircling them both, like a hangman's noose, was a dense wood of dark pine trees.

None of them had ever seen houses with thatched roofs before. Bandy nudged Cess. 'Here – I told you – them joskins out here really does knit their roofs out of grass!'

'Cut your clack!' snapped Tree, in case Tom turned round and gave him a lamming, but she needn't have bothered. Tom wasn't harkening to any of them; he wasn't hearing anything but the silence.

'What's this place called, Turnip?' Tree asked, to break the tension.

'Darkling,' Tom grunted. 'Darkling Deeps.'

'They could have picked summat a bit more cheery.' Tiddy Doll was just saying out loud what they were all thinking.

But Tom ignored her.

130

'Something ain't right down there,' he said. They could all see the fear in Tom's face, and it was making them shiver. But none of them knew – because he'd told no one about the Blood Moon – that what he was dreading to find down there was Death.

CHAPTER 16

So this is how it ends, Stick was thinking, as he struggled to keep his head above the surging water. *Just when I was starting to trust her!*

He was certain sure his short life was going to finish up with him drowndead in the depths of the Thames.

Stick had heard tell that when you were drowning, you saw all the days of your life flash in front of you. But it seemed to him that he hadn't had his fair share of days yet, and he would have liked a lot more.

Fly's tiger never tried to kill her . . . he thought bitterly. *Why did I have to end up with this shifty old scorcher?*

But just at that moment a huge foot loomed above him. The tip of a talon delicately caught hold of the belt of his kecks and fished him from the river, before dumping him down on the riverbank. He lay there on his belly, gasping like a landed trout.

'I'm so terribly sorry!' The dragon was peering at him anxiously. Her warm tongue slithered out and licked him, and this time he didn't feel like she was tasting him. 'I do apologise . . . I didn't mean to . . .'

'You didn't mean to kill me?' Stick snapped.

'That would have been most ungracious,' protested the dragon. 'After you had helped me . . . There is such a thing as a code of chivalry, my boy!'

Stick rolled over and looked up. She looked hurt.

'Thing is, ma'am, I never knows where I am with you . . .' he said weakly.

He could feel her hot breath warming him to the marrow of his cold bones. He wanted to believe her.

'Thing is,' he started again, 'you needs to be able to trust your cullies . . .'

He thought wistfully about Fly and Spud and Sparrow, remembering one winter's night when they'd shared a pie round a fire-bucket they'd half-inched from a night-watchman as he slept, hot coals and all. It seemed a long time ago.

The dragon was looking puzzled. 'Cullies?'

133

'You know, ma'am – friends . . .' *But after all*, he thought, *how could she even know what that word meant? What a long, lonely age it must be since she had lost her sisters.*

The dragon snorted dismissively. 'Friends? What bunkum! How could you and I . . .' She stopped. It felt like there was a struggle going on somewhere behind those yellow eyes.

'Well,' she said crossly. 'It is of course most irregular, all this helping each other.'

Another pause.

'The usual way is for the knight to try and stick the dragon with his thingummyjig – you know, his lance – and for the dragon to send him off with a good scorching and his tail between his legs.'

'But I ain't a knight, ma'am,' Stick reminded her. 'We is just two poor creatures stuck in a tunnel together.'

She nodded, but said nothing. There was another – warm – pause. Stick's trousers were drying out nicely.

He went on, encouraged, 'The question is, ma'am, where do we go now?'

A flash of unease. An unmistakable shift in the eyes.

She don't like talking about that, thought Stick.

'Why can't we remain here? There's plenty of room . . .' she wheedled.

'But there ain't nowt in the way of vittles, ma'am,' Stick pointed out. He could hear the dragon's guts grumbling something wicked now.

'True,' she agreed thoughtfully. 'And I must admit, I am getting a little peckish. Could you not pop up there and get me a snossidge?'

'No snossidge is going to fill up your bread-basket for very long, ma'am.'

He needed to get her to tell him why she'd run away. What – or who – had she been so desperate to escape? He had a strong suspicion as to the who but he needed her to tell him why.

'What did you do for prog before you got stuck in that there tunnel?' he asked, trying to make it sound casual. 'Mebbe we could head back to where you came from and get some vittles there.' Such a wave of different expressions washed over her face now that Stick couldn't fathom what she was thinking. If it didn't seem so unlikely, he could have sworn she was blushing. It looked like a blush of deep shame.

'I shan't go back there – never!' She stamped her foot and let out a howl. 'Gadzooks! Now you've made me hurt my paw again! Go away and stop mithering me!'

It was clear Stick was going to have to use a fair old bit of flim-flam and humbug to cod this creature into leading him back to her old lair.

135

'Let me take another gander at your foot, ma'am,' he said soothingly. 'Mebbe it ain't healing right.'

With an ungracious grunt, the dragon crouched back on her belly and held out her injured foot.

Stick whistled as he unwrapped the stained bandage. 'Lawks, ma'am, it ain't half swollen! No wonder you're feeling so gummagy. Let's give it another wash and see what's what.'

He didn't want to go too close to the water's edge as she dipped in her foot, but he could see the clear water becoming stained with pus and blood as the wound reopened.

As he leaned forward and tried to clean it, the dragon winced and yelped.

'God's bodikins! You clod-pate! Do you have to be so cack-handed?'

'Sorry, milady!' Stick peered again more closely. He wasn't in the habit of physicking dragons, but he'd watched wounds go bad before, and he knew that only a poultice could save that foot.

A memory slipped out – of healing hands tending his own scraped knees after he'd fallen over, many years before. He pushed it away.

He straightened up. 'This place where you comes from . . .' The scaly forehead crinkled into a threatening scowl, but he went on quickly, 'I knows you don't want to go back there, but I needs to know – is it somewhere that's outside of the city? Is it countryside, like – where there might be herbs and stuff handy?' If it was the place he thought it was, he knew exactly where the herbs he needed could be found.

'Perhaps . . .' the dragon admitted, grudgingly. 'It is outside the city, certainly.' A flash of suspicion. 'Why do you need to know?'

'Because I needs to make a poultice, with herbs and such like, and I can't get stuff like that round here. You're going to lose your foot, if I don't poultice it up smartish.'

'My poor paw.' The dragon licked sadly at her foot with her long flickering tongue. But then she whimpered. 'But that man! I can't go back home. He tried to make me do bad things, such bad things! Things that an honourable Werme should never do.'

'What things, ma'am? What did he make you do?' He had to get her to tell him.

She looked up and it was definitely shame he could see in her eyes now. 'They were just children . . . little children . . . just morsels really . . . a mere moment in the mouth! So sweet! Like sugared almonds.'

She stopped short when she saw the dawning horror on Stick's face and shook her head quickly. 'Only a couple! I only ate a couple. I left the rest. I knew it was wrong . . . but the temptation! It was his fault! He tempted me, devil that he is!'

Stick thought he was going to lob up his groats there and then.

Is that what had happened to Spud and Sparrow? Had that man snabbled them and taken them back to her lair? Had this beast who he'd befriended – nursed, even – gobbled down the closest thing he'd got to family? The only people left that he'd allowed himself to care about, with Fly gone . . .

But no. He swallowed hard, forced himself to think straight. That couldn't be right. The dragon had been banged up under Smithfield when Spud and Sparrow went missing. So that man, whatever other wickedness he had done, couldn't have fed them to this dragon. Not yet, any road.

He swallowed again to keep down the wambling in his guts.

'He was feeding you?' he demanded. 'Feeding you with little kinchen, with children – is that what you're telling me?'

He remembered what Tree and Cess had said about gutterlings being snabbled off the streets by the woman with a pickaxe for a nose, and he had a deep suspicion that those self-same gutterlings hadn't ended up going to school and eating plum duff three times a day.

The dragon nodded. 'He kept pushing the dear little things down through a hole in the roof. But I swear, I ate no more than two. I knew it was wrong. I told you before, dragons don't eat children . . . it is against the rules, against our ancient code of chivalry. So I left the rest there, in my cave, and I ran away. I never harmed a hair on their heads, I swear!'

She paused and looked at Stick. 'I would so much rather have had a snossidge. Or a crumpet.'

Her eyes were full of pleading, like she was asking for his forgiveness.

'Nobody had ever known I was down there before,' she whined. 'It was so peaceful, before all this started.'

'But what did you do for prog before, ma'am . . .?'

'Prog? Ah, yes, food – well, there was always a stray sheep or a confused cow that fell into the pit, and then I would have a little sleep and another one would fall in, and that kept me going for centuries. And now and then I would take a trip to Smithfield, in the hope of a snossidge. I don't need much,' she added, defensively. 'Cold-blooded, you know – I can go for ages without eating!' It was definitely an attempt at an apology.

Stick took a deep breath. He needed to know more.

'How did that man know you were there? How did he find you?'

'It all started after these workmen . . . they were digging out the clay in the pit above my cave . . . they were always wanting more clay . . .'

'For bricks.' Stick nodded. He was sure now. He knew this place.

'How should I know?' the dragon snapped impatiently. He'd interrupted her, and now she'd started her confession, it was like she couldn't bear to stop. 'They found bones . . .' Something between a sob and a hiccup got in the way.

For the first time Stick started to think maybe the dragon did have a heart to be broken.

'They found the bones of my sisters. They had been buried for centuries, since the earth moved. They had rested there in peace, until those workmen found them. And then they went scurrying off and brought that man . . .' She shuddered, and Stick knew why. 'They brought that horrid man to the pit, to show him the bones.' Then she sniffed. 'I

140

suppose they wanted money. That is the usual way of it with your kind.'

Stick nodded again.

A great tear rolled down into the shallows of the river. 'That man must have heard me . . . heard me weeping for my sisters . . . I was mourning them afresh . . .'

Another sniff.

'In any case, somehow he realised that something was still alive down there.'

Stick reached out and stroked her muzzle. It seemed like it might be the only bit soft enough to feel his hand.

'Thank you, dear boy. Thank you.' She sighed.

'So what did . . . what did Sir Jasper do then?' There was no need to pretend any more that he didn't know who she was talking about.

'He sent all the workmen away, and after that he got some strange little fellow to come and dig every day with a trowel and a little brush. I could hear him – *tap-tap-tap*, *brush-brush-brush* – all day above my head, jabbering incessant nonsense to himself about dinosaurs.

'Dinosaurs!' she scoffed indignantly. 'Pah! Such idiots, that lot were! Brains the size of peas, you know.' She gave a snort of contempt.

'But it was only going to be a matter of time before . . .' She trailed off.

'Before he found you,' Stick finished it for her. 'So that's why you came away?'

'It was the guilt! I couldn't live with the guilt!' Her huge eyes widened. 'He was using those little children as bait, to keep me there until that desiccated little fungus of a man dug down far enough to get me out.'

At last Stick allowed himself to believe her. She'd wept so many woefuls as she spilled out the whole sorry tale that his feet were wading about in pools of her tears. His reluctance to trust the tricksy old creature was finally gone.

'I suppose he thought that if he fed me it would keep me there, even with all the noise from the digging. Maybe he thought I was hungry – he didn't know that I'd been snacking on stray sheep for centuries.

'So yes, I ran away. I ran away so fast I wasn't thinking where I was going. And I got stuck under Smithfield. As you saw. Pah!' A harrumph of wounded dignity. 'A misjudgement. I was somewhat smaller last time I was there . . .'

She went on quickly, 'So now you see why I can't go back there. It is a place full of bad memories.'

'I can see that, ma'am,' replied Stick. It was a place full of bad memories for him, too. 'But if we don't go back, you're going to lose that foot.' He had to persuade her somehow.

But the dragon wasn't listening. 'I shudder to think what he is planning to do if he should catch me. Put me on show, alive or dead, I should think.'

She sounded a bit peevish now, like an old lady interrupted in the middle of a particularly complicated bit of crochet.

'It's not as if I mind being dead. After all these centuries, to tell you the truth, I'm very weary of being alive. But I don't want that man boiling me down and making money out of my bones.'

'I can see that, ma'am,' Stick said again. He remembered that poor old Megy-lo-snorus put on show and sold by the shilling, and he knew he would do anything to stop this cantankerous old beast ending up like that – being giggled and gawped at by fools. *They ain't doing that to my dragon*, he thought.

There was a long pause, as the dragon eyed him anxiously.

At last Stick stood up and went and rested the palm of his hand on her huge chest, where he thought her heart might be, if she had one. He didn't rightly know why he was doing it, but he put his other hand on his own heart. It just felt like it was what a knight would do.

'Listen, ma'am,' he said. 'I'll go back with you, and we'll face that evil man together, you and me,' he vowed.

The dragon bent her head, like a queen accepting her knight's allegiance.

'And mebbe you can give him a good roasting,' Stick finished, 'and together we'll put an end to his wickedness, for once and for all.'

PART TWO

GOING HOME

CHAPTER 17

Darkling Deeps felt like the loneliest, emptiest place on earth, when the gutterlings walked into the village. The doors of the low white-washed cottages gaped open, swinging on broken hinges. Some of the houses were in ruins, their thatched roofs charred and their walls black with soot.

There were no mothers sunning themselves on the steps, no children rolling marbles in the gutter. The wide high street was deserted. Not a cart, not a horse, not a soul in sight. Just eerie silence.

'Ma!' Tom tore off up the street, not caring who came with him.

The gutterlings followed more slowly. No one said a word. They were all twitched. Even though there was nobody to be seen, it felt like something – or someone – was watching every step they took up the echoing street.

When they caught up with Tom, he was standing staring, white-faced, at one of the burned-out cottages. He took a step forwards and pushed cautiously at the remains of the red door, which looked like it had been smashed in with an axe.

A ball of hissing, spitting fury leaped out at them.

'Bust me!' swore Bandy, jumping swiftly backwards.

'Ginger!' Tom squatted down to rub the ears of a bedraggled, bony cat. It crept into his arms and he buried his face in its fur.

'He don't want us to see that he's wet around the winkers,' observed Tree, quietly, to her sister.

Cess nodded. 'What in tarnation's happened here?'

'Where's Ma?' Tom was whispering into the cat's ear. He turned to Tree. 'She'd never have left her Ginger! Pa always said Ma loved that cat more than the whole boiling lot of us put together.'

He put Ginger down gently and straightened up, before pushing again at the door. It swung open with a screech of twisted hinges that echoed around the empty street, making them all jump and look quickly round. Gutterlings like them, bred to be always on the lookout for the crushers, had

148

a sixth sense about when they were being watched, and none of them felt easy.

'Hold up – you're not going in there on your lonesome.' Tree felt for Tom's hand and together they disappeared into the dark cottage.

Before she followed them both inside, Cess turned back to Bandy. 'Here, Bandy, you stand stall out here and shout if anyone comes. I don't but half trust this havey-cavey place. I reckon somebody don't want nobody poking about round here.'

Leaving Bandy on the lookout, she and Tiddy Doll stepped inside.

'Pize take it!' Cess swore. 'What a pandalorum!'

The few bits of furniture were either burned or smashed to bits. A thick layer of ash covered the floor. Rags of once-cheerful red gingham curtains fluttered like wounded birds at the windows, and charred, sodden thatch wept from the roof. There was no sound but the scurrying of rats' feet.

In spite of the devastation, Tree felt Tom's grip on her hand relax and she gave it a squeeze. She could guess what he had been afraid to find in here.

The rest of them shuffled and stared at their feet awkwardly. They'd none of them ever had a home or a family to lose, but it didn't take much imagining to work out how it must feel.

'Croopus, Tom,' whispered Tiddy Doll. 'Someone really wanted your Ma and Pa gone.'

'Not just them,' croaked a voice. 'The whole village's gone. He drove them all out.'

Staring in at them from the back door, which had been wrenched off its hinges, was a tiny old woman, wilder than any they'd ever seen, even in all their years on the streets. Skin burned brown as a hazelnut, eyes blazing like black coals, and a face as bony as a bird's.

Tiddy Doll backed away towards Cess. 'She's as mad as a maggot!'

'Crazy Molly, they calls her,' Tom whispered to Tree. 'In the village they says she's a witch, just never got round to burning her. Ma won't have any of it, says she's harmless as a day-old chick.'

Molly scuttled towards them like a crab and snatched hold of Tiddy Doll's wrist. 'Kinchen all gone . . . everyone gone, all gone, all gone but me.'

'Cess! Get her off me!' Tiddy Doll struggled to get free.

Tom went over and caught up the clawlike hands that were still clutching at Tiddy. 'Hold up, Molly! It's all rug

150

– you know me, it's Tom. Ma sent me away, but I be come home . . .'

Molly grabbed at his shirt. She was no bigger than a child. 'All alone, all alone!' she was wailing.

'You needs to tell us where they all be gone, Molly.'

'That evil varmint up at Darkling Hall – he drove them all out and set fire to the houses! He's always hated us . . .'

'You means Sir Jasper?' Tom's freckles had abandoned him again. 'He's always been a bad 'un, him and that hatchet-faced sister of his!'

The wild grey snakes of hair nodded along with Molly's head. 'He closed down the brickworks and threw all the men out of work. He's put up a fence round the pit, to keep everyone away . . .'

'Away from the brick pit?'

Molly nodded her head in terror, as if the mention of the brick pit had struck her dumb.

There was a shout from the street outside, where Bandy was keeping watch. 'Tow-row!' All but Tom recognised it as the gutterlings' watchword for trouble. Someone was coming. Someone who meant them no good.

'We needs to get gone, Tom,' hissed Cess urgently.

There was a clatter of hooves outside and confused shouts from Bandy, which were abruptly muffled.

151

'Come on, best mizzle – out the back!' Cess caught hold of Tiddy Doll and headed for the back door. Tree tugged at Tom's shirt.

But he pulled away from her and turned back to Molly. 'What about the childers, Molly, what's he done with all the childers?'

But by now, Molly was just moaning to herself. Tom cupped his hands round her hollowed face to try to get her attention, but he dropped them when he saw the horror in her eyes.

'He's feeding them one by one to Beelzebub down in that brick pit!' she croaked. 'There's nothing but their ghosts left – I has seen them, I has heard their poor lost souls, wandering about down there and calling out for their mothers . . .'

Molly clutched at him, her black eyes blazing with madness and fear. 'Don't you go down to the pit, boy! Get yourself back to the city, out of harm's way.'

But Molly's warning was wasted. And Bandy's shouts from the street had come too late. Bulky figures were blocking out the sun at both doorways, front and back, and before any of the gutterlings could run, they each took a blow to the head.

Thick sacks were thrust over them like candle-snuffers. And after that they knew nothing.

CHAPTER 18

'Lawks, ma'am, it's a fair old step to this blessed roosting-ken of yours!'

It felt like hours since Stick and the dragon had crossed the river. Stick had climbed on to her back and clung like a limpet to the spikes on her spine as she stepped over the torrent. He wasn't taking any chances of another dunking.

The tunnel back to the dragon's lair seemed to go on for ever. Mile after mile, the walls still bearing the marks of her talons where she'd scraped away the bare rock, however many centuries ago. Some places were dry underfoot, some sticky with mud and running wet from an underground spring.

Stick had no recollection of how many miles it was from London back to the place he dreaded so deep in his heart.

He never let himself think about the small boy who'd made

that journey all those years ago. The way he told it in his head, he'd been born in a London gutter at the age of six, and taught himself to tumble the very next day. His name had come later, when he'd been christened 'Stick' by Fly and the gutterlings.

He never let himself think about how he'd made his way to London, either. But whenever he'd caught the smell of sheep brought to market at Smithfield, it had broken down the high wall he'd built around that memory.

It was a memory of being buried snug as a bug beneath a flock of warm, woolly bodies, bleating and jostling to keep their feet in a wooden cart rattling over cobbles. The smell of lanolin on a lamb's fleece always brought it back in an instant. Sheep meant safety.

Stick's feet had picked up on the dread his heart was feeling, and he realised he was getting slower with every step. But it wasn't just him that was dawdling. He gave the dragon's flank a playful slap, to gee her up.

'Chin up, old girl! We won't get there in a month of Sundays at this rate.'

She reared her great snout with a harrumph of offended dignity. 'Have some respect for your elders, hedge-fish! I'll have you know I was carving out my tunnels under London for centuries, until that Julius Caesar came along and mucked it all up by putting in his fancy underground

154

heating everywhere.' She was back on her high horse after her snivelling confession.

'Don't rightly know no coves by that name, ma'am, but I do know that we've been going slower than a snail's gallop for the past half-hour. And if we carries on at this rate, the rot's going to set in to that foot of yours something wicked. And there'll be no herbs I knows about what could save it then.'

She picked up the pace a bit after that, limping along in affronted silence.

Stick clamped his pipe between his teeth. Normal-times, Stick preferred to save his tobaccoless pipe-smoking for moments of calm consideration. But this wasn't normal-times, and Stick had a parcel of problems to apply to his pipe.

I still ain't no closer to finding Spud and Sparrow, which is how all this blame-fool business started, he thought.

Even though the gutterlings always swore that he was the cunning one, the one that was dabs at sorting out problems, Stick was starting to think it had been a buffle-headed notion to set out on this malarkey without Tree and Cess and the rest of them. *What the dickens is I going to do when I gets there, any road?* He hadn't got even the ghost of a plan.

He would have worried even worse if he'd known that the gutterlings had set out after him, only to be snabbled themselves in the very village he and the dragon were heading towards.

It was the smell that told Stick they'd finally arrived at the dragon's home. As the stagnant tunnel opened into a huge cavern, a breeze of fresher air brought a smell that was

a curious combination of burned bricks and wet clay, and a hint of the distant Thames blown in over the salt-marshes. And with it came the unmistakable smell of pine trees.

Someone had once told Stick that pine trees killed everything that tried to grow beneath them. To this day, he hated the smell of pine trees. That's what he liked about London. Nothing but the comfortingly familiar smell of sewers and unwashed bodies.

Before he could stop it, another memory slipped out of the cupboard. That cupboard, which he'd kept locked for so long, was starting to leak like a sieve.

In this memory, he was being held safe in someone's arms, looking down from the top of a tower through dense, dark pine-woods, towards the red glow of the brickworks, which burned night and day.

'Is that Hell down there?' he'd asked, because he'd heard about Hell at Sunday School. The someone who was holding him had laughed and said no, and not to worry because Hell was a very long way away.

'Turns out you was mistook,' muttered Stick, without letting himself think about who he was talking to.

The dragon waddled wearily into the cave and flopped down on her belly. Home sweet home. She didn't look too happy about it.

'Now what?' she snapped. She was clearly feeling as jumpy as a barrel of weasels. Just like Stick.

Sunlight crept through cracks in the roof above. Stick judged it must be late afternoon by the hollow where his guts should be.

There was a steady tap-tapping of metal on the rock above their heads. *Tap-tap-tap. Brush-brush-brush.*

She sighed. 'That pesky fellow is still at it up there.' She

158

stretched out her bad foot petulantly and gave Stick a vicious kick, almost knocking him off his feet. 'Blame it! My foot really hurts now! You made me do all that walking. You said you were going to mend it, and you have just made it worse!' She squinted at him with the eye closest to him. 'If you don't mend it, I shall eat you.'

'Don't start all that again, ma'am,' Stick retorted. 'I ain't going to fall for your flim-flam no more.'

The dragon pouted sulkily and curled up with her tail over her snout like an enormous spiky cat, so Stick left her and set off to explore the cave. Truth be told, he'd been half-hoping that Spud and Sparrow had found their way here through the tunnel somehow, and they'd be lolling around with their feet up, demanding to know what had kept him. But there was no sign of them.

There was something else worrying him, though. He had a good ferret around, but all he could see were piles of old dragon dung. It didn't add up.

If all them childers were chucked down here with no vittles, sure as eggs is eggs they'd have starved to death by now. He didn't really want to think about it, but he reckoned there should either be bones or bodies or some very, very hungry children.

He went back to the dragon and gave her a poke. Her

eyelids were almost closed, but he knew she'd been watching him.

'Thing is, ma'am, if you only ate a couple of childers, where's the rest of them gone?' he demanded.

The dragon yawned, but kept her eyelids firmly shut, so he couldn't see if she was hiding any lies. 'I really wish you would stop mithering me with dreary little details.'

'I needs you to tell me the truth, ma'am!' Stick said sternly. 'The whole truth.'

'Very well. Maybe I ate three.' The eyelids slid open. 'But then one of the others started shouting at me, telling me I should be ashamed of myself, eating small children. Pretty little thing she was, with ginger curls and an excess of ribbons, but far too opinionated for her own good. Anyway, that reminded me about the ancient rules. The code of chivalry and not eating defenceless children . . . so I stopped. Eating them, that is.'

A long sigh.

'I expect they climbed out somehow after I'd left. I'm glad they've gone. Especially that one. She was very noisy. Good riddance, I say.'

The dragon's face took on the same expression Spud had when he was thinking about meat pies. 'Although she did look rather tasty.' The forked tongue slipped out and slithered along her thin, reptilian lips. 'Now, hurry along and find those herbs you keep wittering on about . . .' She gave a wide yawn. 'And do bring back some crumpets, dear boy.'

She closed her eyes firmly and started to snore. Stick had noticed she had a way of taking refuge in sleep when it didn't suit her to answer any more questions.

He looked at her, and then he looked at the foot she'd kicked him with a few moments before. The wound was swollen to the size of a barrel of oysters and was leaking green and yellow pus. And, as far as it was possible to tell with a dragon, her craggy forehead looked decidedly flushed and feverish between the scales.

He didn't have the faintest shadow of a fully formed plan. But first things first, he needed to climb out of the cave somehow and find those herbs, or he'd have a dead dragon on his hands. Aside from the fact that he had to admit he was becoming quite fond of the old blubber-belly, he was going to need her help if he was ever going to defeat that evil man.

CHAPTER 19

Tap-tap-tap. Brush-brush-brush. Tap-tap-tap.

The tapping of hammer against stone grew louder as Stick scrambled up the sloping side of the cave, towards a shaft of light he had spotted earlier. He was hoping, as his bare toes wriggled about in search of footholds, that the children who had been thrown down there as dragon bait had escaped the same way.

All but three of them, any road, if the old curmudgeon ain't still lying like a flat fish. The memory of the dragon dribbling about sugared almonds distracted him just as he was tackling a steep bit, and his foot slipped.

'Bust me!' His toehold crumbled, sending a shower of stones cascading down and leaving him dangling from his fingertips like a Christmas turkey in a butcher's shop window.

The tapping stopped. Stick froze. *Drabbit it!* he thought. *That cove up there's twigged there's something moving about down here.*

'Tarnation!' he swore under his breath. 'I ain't rightly sure how long me dib-dabs can hang on up here.'

He knew nothing about the man who'd been given the job of digging up the dragon, but if he was anything like the master he served, Stick was in no hurry to make his better acquaintance. His plan had been to sneak past him, quiet as a house-breaker climbing in through a toff's windy. Sparrow – who'd been apprenticed to a burglar until he'd turned tumbler – had taught Stick and Spud a trick or two about getting in and out of places they had no lawful right to be in, skills that had oftentimes come in handy before now.

It seemed like an age before the tap-tapping started again, and even then, there were long silences in between taps, as if somebody was pausing to listen. Cautiously, Stick set off again up the slippery slope, stopping every time the tapping stopped. It was a game of cat and mouse, making for painfully slow progress.

At last he reached the top, and all that remained was for him to poke his head out, like a coney out of its burrow. He propped himself more securely, just below the surface, and waited. Above him, the light was turning a pinkish-gold,

163

and Stick reckoned that by now the late August sun must be dipping below the rim of the pit. The tapping had stopped again.

Mebbe he's knocked off for a bite of supper, Stick thought.

He waited a little longer anyway, just to be safe, watching a clump of tall grasses above him tossing in the evening breeze. Something was caught on the clump closest to the edge and he reached out for it. It was a little green and white gingham ribbon. The sort of ribbon that a mother might think looked well amongst her daughter's ginger curls.

Stick gave a low whistle. *Mebbe the old scorcher ain't such a liar, arter all. Mebbe that little bossy one got away. Unless of course her ribbon got caught on the grass when Sir Jasper pushed her down.*

He shivered, though it wasn't cold, and carefully tucked the ribbon away in what was left of his scorched pocket.

He was just about to poke his head out when he heard the sound of heavy feet approaching, crushing small stones in their path.

If stones could speak, they'd be crying out in pain, Stick thought. It was someone very large, who cared nothing about what – or who – they trampled underfoot.

It was the voice, though, that confirmed Stick's fears. That booming voice, swelling up from a beer-barrel of a chest – the voice that no one had ever dared to defy, the voice that had filled his childhood with terror.

'Well, Scrope? Have you found the beast?'

A squeak of alarm.

That don't sound like someone who could stand up to Sir Jasper. Stick didn't know how the tap-tapper had ended up in this man's clutches, but he pitied him, even before he'd made his acquaintance.

'How much longer are you going to be fossicking about down here with your foolish little trowels?'

Another squeak of alarm. Stick smelled fear, and he wasn't sure if it was coming from the tap-tapper or from himself.

There was an ominous rumble, like gathering thunder, in Sir Jasper's deep chest. 'I am not a patient man! I cannot wait for ever!'

'But, Sir Jasper, you cannot hurry science . . .'

Stick held his breath. *He ain't going to like that.*

'Palaeontology is in its infancy, my lord – we must not risk losing even the tiniest fragment of evidence. The smallest slip of my hammer could destroy the work of millennia! If by some miracle we have found a live specimen, we must proceed with extreme caution. We had an agreement – you promised to give me time to investigate properly if I helped you.'

Stick couldn't help but admire the tap-tapper's courage. *He's braver than I gave him credit for.* But he knew it couldn't end well.

'Fiddlesticks to palaeontology!' roared Sir Jasper. 'You have been scratching away down here for weeks. I'm not paying you to play at sandcastles with your little bucket and spade while my brickworks stand idle. Time is money, man. And money means meat!'

Stick braced himself for the crunch of one of those great fists cracking Scrope's skull like a new-laid egg. He'd seen it done. He'd felt the force of those fists himself. But the crunch didn't come.

'But there is good news, my lord!' There was a frisson of excitement in the reedy, quivering voice. 'I detected sounds down there this afternoon. I believe the beast has returned.'

'Drabbit it! You addle-pated jobberknoll! It's back? Why didn't you say so?'

A loud thump followed, which Stick reckoned was the threatened smack on the head being turned into a congratulatory clap on the back. There was a stifled gasp of pain.

That Scrope chap don't sound like he's a cove what could take much of a beating, Stick was thinking.

166

'This changes everything . . . the beast will be mine, all mine . . . it is only a matter of time . . .'

There it was – that unmistakable gurgle of greed, catching in his throat. Stick had a sudden memory of a child watching in horrid fascination over a dinner table, as Sir Jasper tore apart the carcass of some barely cooked animal and stuffed it almost whole into his cavernous maw.

'Keep going, keep going, Scrope! But I am warning you, if you don't find the beast by tomorrow evening, I will be back with a dozen boxes of dynamite.'

'But, Sir Jasper, the beast would die!'

'Why should I care? I cannot wait any longer – it might disappear again!' A bark of laughter. 'Besides, even if we cannot take it alive, its bones will still be worth their weight in gold when I put them on show.'

Stick could hear those bloated, red hands, like slabs of raw meat with thick sausages for fingers, being rubbed together in greedy anticipation. Just when Stick thought he was done, Sir Jasper spoke again, in a chilling tone, 'But I shall be sure to get a taste of its heart first.'

Stick knew in that moment that he would do anything to stop this man getting those hands on his dragon.

'Best keep digging, Scrope, if you want to save your precious specimen.' Sir Jasper was leaving.

167

Stick could hear him talking to himself as his heavy footsteps crunched away. 'The beast will be hungry after its travels. It will need fresh food. My sister was right to keep collecting those guttersnipes, after all – in spite of how much it has cost us to keep them alive. We will throw more of them down as bait in the morning. It cannot be allowed to escape us again.'

Stick swallowed hard to keep his queasy stomach in its place. So it wasn't only the dragon that Stick had to save from this man. It was also the gutterlings that Sir Jasper and his sister had snatched from the streets – and Stick was sure now that Spud and Sparrow must be among them.

Silence descended on the brick pit after the sound of Sir Jasper's boots faded, but it was a while before Stick let himself breathe again. There was no more tap-tapping to be heard.

Mebbe he's packed up for the day, thought Stick. *Poor old codger, more than likely needs a nice lie-down after all that.*

But before he could climb up, a thin reedy voice quavered right above his head. 'You can come out now, he's gone.'

Stick's first instinct was to slither straight back down to the dragon. But before he could escape, a bewhiskered, dusty kind of face, with small, brown eyes that looked like they might more properly belong to a dormouse, appeared between the tall grasses.

'There is no cause for alarm. Sir Jasper truly is gone. I thought it wise not to alert him to your presence.'

Stick spluttered. 'How did you twig?'

'Twig? Ah yes, you mean how did I deduce you were there? Oh, we palaeontologists are trained observers of detail, my boy. Whilst Sir Jasper was talking – or perhaps I should more accurately describe it as shouting – I noted a regular disturbance of the grasses, betokening the inhaling and exhaling of some living creature. Too large to be a rabbit, and too small to be – well, too small to be the thing I am searching for.'

Scrope peered at Stick as if he was some sort of palaeontological exhibit. 'I have become alert to the smallest of changes in this ancient place. Was it you that caused the disturbance of those small stones, most likely from the Jurassic period, earlier?'

Stick nodded, and the sandy whiskers drooped in disappointment, mixed with not a little fear. 'Ah, I think perhaps I gave false encouragement to Sir Jasper?'

Stick grinned. 'Got him off yer back, though, mister.'

'Indeed.' A slight twitch of the whiskers. 'It did, indeed, give temporary relief. I deduce from your hesitation to emerge that you have a reluctance to be seen by Sir Jasper?'

Stick nodded.

'Probably very sensible. But you need have no anxiety now. He will not be back until the morning.' A look of unease crossed Scrope's face. 'I fear Sir Jasper may not be altogether a gentleman.'

He stopped and sighed, then the dusty whiskers perked up again. 'Perhaps you would care to come and take tea with me? It is such a long time since I had company. And I believe my charlady has left crumpets today. It is always crumpets on a Wednesday. Do you partake of crumpets?'

'Mister, if "partake" is a fancy way of saying "does I eat crumpets?" – then don't I just!'

Stick was not one to shilly-shally when there was the prospect of prog, and he pulled himself out of that hole in two shakes of a lamb's tail.

'Boil me!' he observed to himself as he followed Scrope out of the pit. 'What is it with everyone and crumpets today?'

CHAPTER 20

It was hours since the heavy oak door had last opened on the foul-smelling underground place in which the street urchins had been imprisoned. Hours since they had last been fed.

At last the key turned in the lock and the light flooded in. Towering in the doorway was the woman who had seduced them all off the streets with the promise of school and three meals a day. She was a giant of a woman, and she had a nose that would have looked more at home on a vulture.

'Here, missus, what about that plum duff?' Squinty never stopped hoping, every time the key sounded in the lock and the door swung open, that this time there would be pudding. But as Tree and Cess had suspected, Squinty had no more wit than a coot.

All the other gutterlings locked up down there had given up on plum duff long ago. Most of them had given up on getting out of there alive.

'Are you still snivelling, snotty-nose?' the woman sneered. A powerful kick sent Squinty sprawling down the stone steps. 'Get out of my way!'

'Coo, what a conk!' someone whispered, but very softly. Her prisoners had learned to avoid her boots – and the big stick she brandished to stop any of them making a break for freedom.

'Throw the new brats down!' she ordered. A pair of stocky manservants dragged five tightly bound bundles to the top of the steps and tossed them down. The bundles bounced to the bottom. There was a sickening crack of bone on stone as the smallest one landed.

The sacks lay there wriggling like maggots – all but the little one, which lay ominously still.

'You can rot there until tomorrow, you dirty guttersnipes! How dare you snoop around, interfering in my brother's affairs!' Her voice grated like a bit of cinder trapped under a door. 'You'll be sorry you ever set foot in Darkling Deeps, when you see what's waiting for you in that pit!

'Feed the rest of them!' she barked at the men.

'Yes, ma'am.' The men, dressed in some sort of servant's uniform, jumped to her command, and a pot of something that stank worse than ten-day-old tripe was hurriedly thrust in, followed by metal bowls that tumbled down the steps.

'That's the closest to plum duff you'll be getting, you fool!' She slammed the heavy oak door shut, and the darkness returned.

A loud sniff from Squinty. 'It don't smell nothing like plum duff.'

'Bust me!' came Tree's voice from one of the bundles. 'Is that Squinty? Is you still blethering on about plum duff, you nick-ninny?'

'I told you he was daffy!' It was Cess talking now, from inside another bundle.

'Blimey – that ain't Cess, is it? And Tree?' said another voice in the dark.

The voice sounded familiar to Cess. 'Spud? Is that you?'

'Yeah!'

'And me!' Sparrow's voice chipped in.

'How did you end up down here?' It was Tree's voice again.

'Some cove with a face like a beetroot snabbled us at Bartlemy Fair,' replied Spud. 'Knocked us on the head with his umbyrelly, but I reckon he'd got a piece of lead piping hidden inside. Didn't wake up 'til we was chucked down here in a big sack together.'

'Is Stick with you?' demanded Sparrow.

173

'Never mind all that!' Bandy's muffled voice spluttered. 'They've got us trussed up like chickens in here! Get us out, before we is sufflicated!'

Spud produced a knife and felt his way around the bundles to find the ropes that had been tied tight around them.

'Ouch! Watch out! That's me leg, cabbage-head!'

'It's darker than a whale's belly down here, in case you hadn't noticed!' Spud retorted. 'I is doing my best!'

'Ain't no one got a glim?' Cess rubbed her numb limbs after Spud finally managed to cut her free.

'I has!' offered Squinty. There was the sound of a Lucifer match striking, and a circle of baffled and furious faces was revealed in the quivering light of a candle stub.

'Why didn't you say you had a light?' Sparrow spluttered. 'We has been sitting here in the dark!'

Squinty shrugged. 'You didn't ask.'

Tree sighed. 'Dunderhead!'

Nobody noticed, in the half-light, that the smallest of the bundles was still not moving.

'What about this prog, then?' Tom staggered to his feet and went to sniff at the pot the manservants had dragged in. 'If it is prog? Never smelled nowt like it.'

Spud was staring at Tom. He nudged Tree. 'Who's the country splodger with all the questions?'

'We calls him Turnip Tom,' Cess butted in.

'It's just Tom, now,' Tree scowled at her sister. 'He's one of us.'

One of the street urchins who'd been there a while answered Tom. ''Tis the same old maw-wallop they been feeding us all week. Fish-porridge.'

'But there ain't any fish . . .' added Sparrow.

'And there ain't a lot of porridge . . .' finished Spud.

Whatever it was in the pot, it was soon gone. After they'd finished scraping their bowls, Tree looked round at their fellow prisoners. It was difficult to count up who was there in the small circle of light from the candle, but apart from Squinty, Spud and Sparrow, there were at least half a dozen gutterlings she recognised from the streets, and some other children she'd never seen before.

'So that posh dona codded all you nick-ninnies into getting in her carriage, did she?' she scolded.

Cess joined in. 'Promised you all pudding, did she? That old buzzard had you all for flats!'

'We was hungry!' protested one of the girls.

There was no answer to that.

'Was there ever any lessons, like she promised?' asked Bandy.

'First day we got here we had a lesson,' said one of the girls at the back. 'We was in a big room upstairs, and we even had breakfast . . .'

'And that old dona what brought us here, she started teaching us some tosh about the Earth being like a ball what goes round and round the sun,' one of the boys chipped in.

Another of the boys picked up the story. 'And that's when we knew she was lying like a flounder, because anyone can see the Earth is flat and the sun goes sideways-like.'

The first girl continued indignantly, 'So I says to her, don't talk daft, missus, but then she got all fratchety and boxed me ears.'

'And then some cove with a red waistcoat and a face to match, he comes in and he says, "Gertrude, you are wasting time and money . . . Lock them in the crypt until we need them".' One of the boys imitated Sir Jasper's booming voice and everyone giggled, in spite of the pickle they were in.

'That's the cove what snabbled us!' exclaimed Sparrow. 'One minute we was scoffing a nice bit of fried fish with Stick, then we gets a bang on the bonce.'

'And we wakes up down here in the dark with this lot,' Spud added.

'And then Squinty turns up, gay as a goose in a gutter,'

Sparrow finished. ''Cos that woman's promised him plum duff three times a day . . .'

'. . . But there never was no plum duff,' finished Squinty sadly.

'Of course there weren't!' Tree scolded him. 'We warned you!'

'But what does they want with us?' demanded Bandy. 'Why is they keeping us all locked up down here?'

'Dunno,' said one of the boys at the back.

There was a silence.

Tom had said nothing since they'd finished the food. He ran his fingers through his ginger curls, which were so matted with dirt by now they were sticking up like a paintbrush. 'I don't know neither, but whatever it is, it bain't good. They took half the kinchen from my village. My little sister, too. Nobody's seen hide nor hair of them since.'

'We needs to get out of here,' said Tree.

'Don't you think we've tried?' protested Sparrow. 'There's no way out. Be easier to break out of Newgate!'

'We needs Stick!' Spud said. 'Where the blazes is he? Why didn't he come looking for us, along with you?'

Tree and Cess looked at each other and shrugged. 'He just upped and offed in the middle of the night. We ain't seen him since.'

183

'Don't he even care about us?' There was real hurt in Sparrow's voice. 'We'd never have left him to rot down here! When Fly went missing, he had half London out looking for her.'

'None of this chinwagging be getting us out of here.' Tom said impatiently. He picked up the dwindling stub of candle and set off to explore. The rest of the gutterlings trailed after him, their shadows shivering on the dank stone walls. Nobody wanted to be left alone.

'What is this place, Tom?' asked Tree.

'I dunno – I bain't never been inside Darkling Hall afore.' Tom shook his head. 'No one from the village comes up here, if they can help it. No one wants owt to do with Sir Jasper, nor his sister, Gertrude. But I reckon we be in the crypt that used to be under the old chapel, afore Sir Jasper knocked it down.'

'It's a right mirksy, creepy sort of place.' Cess was shivering, but it wasn't because she was cold.

'It don't smell too good, neither,' added Tree.

Nobody liked to say so, but it smelled of nothing so much as death.

The wick was burning low, and Tom cursed and shook hot wax from his fingers. 'This glim bain't going to last much longer. We needs to keep looking. '

In the centre of the dank, gloomy place was a low stone tomb. They all gave it a wide berth, as they looked around for an exit. Nobody said so, but they all feared the heavy lid might lift at any moment and the ghost of whoever lay inside might emerge. Nobody wanted to go near that tomb somehow. Even if any of the gutterlings had been able to read, there was no name nor date on its blank sides to record whose body lay inside. Whoever was buried in there, Sir Jasper clearly didn't want anyone to remember them.

The candle was almost gone by the time they'd finished exploring. They all looked at each other.

'Sparrow's right, there ain't no way out, is there?' Bandy was the one that put their despair into words.

Tom shook his head. 'Only that big wooden door, and they're not going to let us out of there in a hurry.'

They all trailed back to sit in silence on the steps, waiting for the candle to burn out.

'Hold on,' said Cess, looking round the circle. 'Where's Tiddy Doll?'

Tree counted up. Herself, Bandy, Cess and Tom. One missing.

'Tiddy!' There was something awful in Cess's voice as she rushed back to the bottom of the steps. There, lying terribly still in the shadows, was the smallest of the bundles. It hadn't moved since Spud had cut the ropes around it.

Cess stopped, looking down at the little heap of sacking, like she couldn't bring herself to get any closer. Tree squeezed her sister's hand and then kneeled down next to the bundle, gently drawing the coarse hessian cloth to one side.

'No! My Tiddy!' A cry went up from Cess that echoed mockingly around the stone chamber.

'Tiddy . . . Tiddy . . .'

Cess fell to her knees beside her sister.

Tiddy's small face stared up at the gutterlings with eyes the colour of violets, but she saw nothing. That face, which was always looking up and smiling, like a flower seeking out the sun, was now as white and still as the face of a china doll.

'They've broken her!' Cess hugged the little flower-girl to her chest.

She'd looked out for Tiddy like a mother for years, since she and Tree had found her starving and wailing in a gutter. But no matter how tight Cess held her now, she couldn't squeeze the life back into her.

'Them devils has broken Tiddy Doll!' she sobbed.

And then the candle went out.

CHAPTER 21

'Cor, that's better than a slap in the face with a wet fish.' Stick sighed with satisfaction. 'Them is prime crumpets, mister!'

He'd barely taken a breath between mouthfuls – he was now about to start his eighth crumpet and Scrope was eyeing him nervously while nibbling on the edge of his first, as if he thought Stick might soon start on him.

It was only when the butter oozed out of the little holes and dribbled down Stick's chin, congealing in glistening yellow spots on his knees, that he remembered there was someone else who was depending on him for crumpets. And for her life.

He paused guiltily, with the crumpet half-way to his mouth. 'There ain't any more, is there?'

Scrope lifted a clean, white cloth to reveal another plump batch. 'My charlady appears to believe I have the appetite of an African elephant, which I understand consumes a third more than its Asian cousin. I normally resort to concealing them under my mattress. Crumpets, that is, not elephants. Shall I toast you another?'

Stick stuffed in crumpet number eight and stood up to leave, nodding. 'I can do you a favour and take a few off your hands, when I go,' he volunteered. He needed to get gone – he still had the herbs to pick. *Best picked at sunset, when they have taken in the healing power of the sun . . .* That's what someone had told him a long time ago.

'Oh, please don't rush off, dear boy – it is weeks since I spoke to a soul apart from Sir Jasper.' As Scrope turned to toast another crumpet on the fire, Stick heard him add quietly, 'Although it is questionable whether that man even has a soul.'

Stick sat down again. Another crumpet wouldn't hurt. It was the first time he'd eaten since that saveloy, and the gnawing beast in his belly finally gave him peace long enough to take a proper look at the rum cove who was cooking his ninth crumpet.

He'd known from the moment he'd clapped eyes on him that Scrope could be trusted. He reckoned that the little man was as much a victim of Sir Jasper as the rest of them, and probably as much in need of rescuing as the dragon.

Scrope had called himself some long word – 'paley-something' – when he was talking to Sir Jasper, and Stick had no idea what that meant, but he thought Scrope looked like nothing more than a bedraggled bat. He was wearing a billowing black gown over a suit that might once have been black too, and both clothes and man were covered with fine dust and smudges of clay. In fact, everything in the cottage was covered in fine dust, as if Scrope himself was in danger of disintegrating like a fossil.

I've been in this cottage before, Stick remembered. *Some crispy little cove who was in charge of the ovens lived here. He looked like he'd been roasted along with the bricks.*

Stick had that wambling in his guts again, and it wasn't just from a superfluity of crumpets. He had an image of himself as a small boy, his arm gripped by a hand as big as a ham, being dragged through dark pine-woods up to the brickworks. Wailing all the way, for fear of those roaring ovens, which he'd convinced himself were the mouth of Hell.

But when he and Scrope had walked past the brickworks earlier, those same ovens that he had feared so much were standing cold and empty. The long, low drying sheds were abandoned, and the shouts of brick-workers had been replaced by the cawing of black ravens circling over their heads.

Why had Sir Jasper closed the brickworks? What would persuade a man of his greed to give up the fortune he made from selling the bricks?

Scrope, his back still bent over the toasting fork, interrupted his thoughts.

'You remind me of Sir Jasper . . .'

Stick jumped back to his feet and his plate shattered to pieces on the tile floor. 'I ain't like him! I ain't!'

Scrope looked astonished. 'Only in the matter of appetite, dear boy, only in the matter of appetite!' He bent down to pick up the shards of china.

Scrope was enjoying having company too much to notice what a twitch Stick was in, and he went on, in his same mild, dusty manner, 'Sir Jasper once boasted to me that there wasn't a beast in the animal kingdom that he had not tasted. Rather like Noah, except Sir Jasper eats them all rather than saving them from the Flood. He told me so many stories . . . some perhaps I would rather not have heard . . .'

Stick shuddered. He was remembering those stories, too. It was with some difficulty that his belly was holding down his barrow-load of crumpets. He swallowed hard to try to keep his guts in their proper place.

Scrope had still not noticed that Stick had gone deadly white about the gills. 'A curious man, Sir Jasper,' he went on. 'He told me that he once ate the heart of a saint, which had been kept locked up for centuries as a relic at the village church. Tasted like well-hung game, he said. Apparently the priest was most put-out.'

He looked up, startled, as Stick made a dash for the door. 'Are you quite well, my boy?'

At the sound of Stick lobbing his groats up outside, he shook his head sadly. 'Ah, a surfeit of crumpets. I thought that quantity might prove unwise . . .

'Perhaps some camomile tea?' he offered as Stick returned.

But Stick was raging. 'How can you work for that man? Don't you know that he's throwing little childers down into that pit? He's the Devil – the Devil incardinate! And an ediccated man like you should be ashamed of his-self!'

Scrope had turned as white as Stick under his whiskers. 'I didn't know, I assure you, I didn't—'

'You must have known something!'

'Sir Jasper didn't tell me what he was doing,' Scrope protested. 'I was helping him in the interests of science. He put an advert in *The Times* – 'WANTED.

PALAEONTOLOGIST' – well, my boy, that's not something you see every day, as you can imagine. I was intrigued . . .'

'Boil me!' Stick, who understood nothing about the trials and tribulations of being a palaeontologist, exploded. 'You must have been a right clod-pate to trust him! He's as fishy as a week-old halibut! The only thing he cares about is money – and food.'

Scrope was looking shaken. 'But I was so excited when he came to see me. He told me he had reason to believe there was a dinosaur living in his brick pit – a living dinosaur! – and he needed my help in finding it. How could I refuse? Just think of the papers I could write – think of the fame! Not a fossil! A living dinosaur!'

But Stick was still fuming. 'She ain't a dinosaur! She's a dragon. And she's a person – well, mebbe not a person, but a living thing, with feelings – and you're helping that horrible man to make money out of her. He's had you for a flat, mister!'

'A flat?'

'A right jobberknoll – a fool. He don't give a stuff for science. He'll kill her in a wink of a cod's eye, once he gets his evil hands on her, you know he will. If he don't blow her up first. And that's arter he's thrown all my friends down there into that pit! He's lower than a snake's belly. And you're helping him.'

The gutterlings would have been gobsmacked if they could have heard him at this moment. Stick had never said so many words at once in his life. And he'd said much more than he'd ever intended. He'd never planned to tell Scrope about the dragon, but it was all out now.

He glared at Scrope, whose dusty black gown was fluttering about him like the feathers of a moulting blackbird.

'I needs my pipe,' Stick growled.

Once outside, he chomped so viciously on his pipe that he bit clean through the stem. 'I ain't like him, I ain't!' This was the second time someone had said he was like Sir Jasper. What had the dragon said back there, under London? *You smell like him . . .*

A sob got strangled in Stick's throat and he tried to spit it out with the words, 'It ain't true. I ain't nothing like him!'

He tossed the pieces of his broken pipe away impatiently. 'Blimey, what a set-out!' he whispered to himself. 'I ain't got much time. That man will be throwing a fresh batch of childers into that cave tomorrow – and I'll lay Spud and Sparrow will be with them. And whatever the cunning old scorcher down there said about not eating no more childers, if she's really hungry, there's no knowing what she'll do.

Besides which, if Scrope doesn't break through to the cave tomorrow, Sir Jasper says he's going to blow the pit to kingdom come. And there'll be nowt left of Spud and Sparrow – even if she ain't ate them by then – and nowt left of the poor old queen but bones.'

Trying to make a plan without the help of his pipe wasn't working, so he went over and picked up the broken stem and stuck it back between his teeth. He tucked the bowl of his pipe in his pocket. It had got him and Fly and the rest of the gutterlings out of many a scrape, and it felt wrong to part with it.

The figure of Scrope appeared anxiously at the doorway, gown flapping, and brandishing the toasting fork. 'Do come back in and have another crumpet, dear boy.'

'Crumpets! That's it!'

Scrope looked startled as Stick seized his free hand and shook it enthusiastically. The pipe had performed its usual magic. He had a plan. It wasn't as much of a plan as he would have liked, but it was a start.

If he could persuade Scrope to pay a nice long visit to the dragon, and take along the rest of his crumpets with him, he could kill two birds with one stone. Because if he made Scrope disappear, Sir Jasper might wait a day or two before blowing up the pit.

188

Stick grinned. The muscles in his face felt stiff, and he realised he hadn't grinned for a long time. *Them crumpets will keep old belly-guts down there happy – and full – for a while,* he thought. *That might give me time to find Spud and Sparrow . . .*

Out loud he said, 'Look, mister, would you like to meet her? A living, breathing dragon, not some dried-up old dinosaur's bones?'

'Butter my whiskers, my boy! Could I really?'

'Easy as winking,' Stick replied, breezily. 'But first, I has to go and find some herbs. And if it ain't too much bother, could you see your way to lending me a shirt?' His own was still wrapped round the dragon's festering foot, and the evening air was growing chilly.

At last he had a plan. But could he make it work in time to save Spud and Sparrow?

CHAPTER 22

'You have betrayed me!'

The dragon was reared up, within a pig's whisper of torching Stick and the palaeontologist to cinders.

'I should never have trusted you! Why have you brought that man down here? You are just like the rest of your kind! Is there no honour left in this world?'

Stick thought that was a bit rich from a beast that clearly would have snaffled him for supper many times over, if he hadn't kept his wits about him. But now wasn't the time to argue.

'I ain't betrayed you, ma'am! We is friends – remember? Look – I has brought the herbs for the poultice, like I promised!'

He brandished a bunch of greenery at her, the herbs

that he had found in the same old familiar places that he had been shown by someone, many years before. He'd had to wipe his eyes as he'd gathered the leaves and roots from the fields near the brick pit, because unaccountably they'd kept filling up and blurring so he couldn't see to pick anything.

'Humph!' The dragon was listening at least, but Stick could see an ominous glow behind her pupils. The furnaces were still stoked, ready to ignite a scorching breath. At one time Stick had thought that was all she had inside. Just burning flames where her heart should be. But now he wasn't sure about that.

'And look, ma'am!' Stick nudged Scrope, who was carrying a load of crumpets in a big bag, and hissed, 'Show her the crumpets, before we both get frazzled to kingdom come!'

Scrope, shaking but mesmerised, opened the bag and showed the contents to the dragon. She sank instantly back down to all fours and sniffed at the bag, so close that she was in danger of snorting it up her nostrils.

Scrope's feet shuffled anxiously, like they weren't sure whether it was safest to stand still or scurry back up the slope.

'Is there butter?' she demanded. Her eyes were still

glinting dangerously.

Scrope was looking more and more confused. And more and more nervous.

He don't twig what she's saying, thought Stick. *Why can I talk to her, and he can't?* He tucked that puzzle away.

'She's asking about the butter,' he explained.

Scrope nodded. 'Yes. Of course. The butter. What was I thinking?' He produced a full pat of butter from one of the voluminous sleeves of his black gown. And a set of bone-handled butter knives and some rather pretty afternoon-tea plates from the other.

'Ah!' breathed the dragon, in deep satisfaction. Her breath was now just comfortably warm, Stick noted with some relief.

'Excellent!'
She subsided
to the ground
and tucked her
feet comfortably
beneath her, looking at
Stick expectantly.

'Shall I toast them?'
she asked.

'If you're careful,' Stick said. 'Not too much
hot, ma'am.'

He laid out the crumpets on a convenient rock and signalled to Scrope to stand back a little.

'Ahhhhhhh . . .' The dragon breathed gently on the row of crumpets and, sure enough, within moments they were toasted golden-brown, nice as ninepence.

'Now butter them, while they're still warm!' she prompted the palaeontologist eagerly. 'And don't hold back!' she snapped at Scrope, who still understood nothing. 'Make it so the butter runs out of those dear little holes.'

'She wants plenty of butter,' interpreted Stick. 'And best be quick about it, sir,' he added, though he didn't really need to, because Scrope was already buttering the crumpets like his life depended on it. Which it probably did.

Once they were buttered to her satisfaction, the crumpets disappeared so fast it seemed as if the dragon was inhaling them rather than actually eating them. When they were gone, she looked longingly at the still-bulging bag that Scrope had brought with him. 'I assume there are more?'

Stick was relieved that he'd got Scrope to dig out all the crumpets he'd hidden from his charlady under the mattress. *I reckon they'll be fine, once they're toasted*, he thought nervously. *She won't notice they ain't so fresh, eating them at that rate!*

Sure enough, the stale crumpets went down just as fast as the fresh ones had. It wasn't until the fourth batch that the dragon paused for breath.

'Well, why *have* you brought him down here?' Shiny yellow butter was dribbling down her scaly green chin. 'This had better be good, gutter-boy!'

Scrope looked at Stick anxiously, even though he didn't know what she was saying. Stick understood his nervousness. Nobody could feel comfortable with ten tons of dragon eyeing them up like that.

'Well, ma'am . . .' *Time for some serious flummery*, thought Stick. 'He wanted to see you so much – he told me as he'd waited all his life to see something as wonderful as you, and I couldn't break his poor old heart by saying "no", now, could I?'

'Humph!' But it was a much gentler humph now, and Stick knew the flummery was working.

'He don't mean you no harm, ma'am – it's Sir Jasper who wants to put you on show, not him. Mister Scrope, he just wanted to get a gander at you in all your wonder. And he wants to help. Besides, he had all these crumpets going begging. And you made me promise to bring you crumpets.'

Scrope was nodding like a calf-lolly, to show he meant no

195

harm. 'It is the greatest honour of my life to meet you, ma'am, indeed, it is the pinnacle of my career!' He bobbed and bowed his head to show his admiration.

To Stick's surprise, the corners of the dragon's mouth twitched upwards, into the beginning of a distinctly self-satisfied smile.

'You can understand him, ma'am?'

'Of course I can. But naturally, he cannot understand me. I explained that to you before – were you not paying attention, you blethering idiot?' she snapped. 'Only a knight can converse with a dragon – heaven only knows why a common sewer-rat like you slipped through the net!'

The common sewer-rat nodded in agreement. 'Can't work that one out myself neither, ma'am.'

Then he nodded at the dragon's foot. 'Why don't I sort out a poultice for that foot of yours, while you woffle down a few more crumpets?'

Best to keep her mouth full, he thought.

The dragon nodded graciously, still smiling at the palaeontologist like a queen giving an audience. Scrope bobbed and bowed from a carefully safe distance.

Stick left Scrope to keep the dragon supplied with buttered crumpets, whilst he found a flat surface and a piece

196

of stone to grind his herbs to a thick, green paste. Then he gingerly unwound what was left of his old shirt from around her foot. The wound was even more swollen than before, and still leaking yellow and green pus. He was glad he'd thought to borrow a new shirt from Scrope. Even a gutterling wouldn't be seen dead on the streets in this one.

The dragon whimpered and spluttered through her latest mouthful. 'It hurts.'

'I know, ma'am. But this will help, if you'll just be brave and hold still for a minute.'

Stick cleaned the wound with fresh cloth he had brought with him, torn from Scrope's bedsheets. 'Not a moment too soon for this poultice, ma'am.'

He was leaning against her flank, and he could feel shudders of pain rippling through her as he pasted on a thick layer of the mixture.

'Your trotter will be fine and dandy in no time, I promise.' He wrapped more of Scrope's landlady's sheets into a bandage, hoping he was telling the truth. Not only because he reckoned he'd be burned to a cinder if he broke his word, but also because he really didn't want his dragon to die. Even if she was the most curmudgeonly and untrustworthy creature he'd ever met.

At last he stepped back. He hesitated. He wasn't sure

197

how she would take the next bit of his plan, even though he had provided her with some company. And a plentiful supply of crumpets.

'You're leaving me, aren't you?' She swung her snout round and knocked Stick off-balance, pinning him against the wall. Her eyes blazed at him.

'Where are you sneaking off to?'

Stick wriggled but he couldn't free himself. He could smell his nice new shirt singeing.

'I have to go and find my friends, ma'am. You remember – I asked you whether you'd eaten them, by accident, like, back when we first met. I knows now that you didn't,' he added hastily, 'because you gave me your word that you don't eat childers no more.'

'But what about me?' the dragon whimpered. 'You can't leave me here all alone.'

She's gone from threats to tears as fast as a dog could lick a dish, thought Stick. He needed to put the wheedle on her, before she cut up rough.

'Not alone, ma'am – that's why I brought this nice Mister Scrope to keep you company, 'til I get back. And there's plenty of crumpets left.'

'It's not just that, though.' The snout sniffed suspiciously at him, like it could sniff out the truth.

198

'You're going to find that man, aren't you? The one who smells like you.'

Stick bit his lip, feeling the colour draining out of his face. He glanced at Scrope, but he'd clearly not understood any of what the dragon had said.

In the end Stick nodded. 'I have to stop him, ma'am,' he said quietly. 'I have to stop him from hurting my friends. And stop him from hurting you.' Stick swallowed hard. 'I can't stop him hurting the people he's already hurt. I can't help the people who are already dead.' His eyes were pricking, and he wiped them angrily with the back of his hand. 'I wasn't old enough before. But I am now. And it's up to me to stop him. And that evil sister of his, Gertrude. But I swear I will come back for you.'

And then he added, 'If I can . . .' under his breath, because he wasn't sure of anything when it came to Sir Jasper. He knew in his heart that he might not be able to keep that promise. He might not be coming back.

The snout retreated, and Stick could breathe again. The dragon turned her back on him, waddled to the far corner of the cave and curled up.

'Go on, then!' came a muffled voice from the snout now buried deep under her bristling tail. She had the air of a scaly and disgruntled green tabby. 'See if I care.'

'You promise me you won't eat Mister Scrope?' insisted Stick. After all, Scrope wasn't a child, and there had never been any mention of a chivalric ban on dragons eating grown men. Even one with whom a dragon had shared afternoon tea.

Scrope twitched and went even paler.

'Why would I eat that desiccated old thing?' retorted the centuries-old dragon. 'I'm sure he would taste of nothing but dust.

'I promise I won't harm a hair on his head.' Then she added, eyes glinting, 'As long as the crumpets last.'

CHAPTER 23

It was dark by the time Stick scrambled out of the small hole at the top of the dragon's lair. He'd not felt entirely comfortable about leaving Scrope down there with the old buzzard, but he had to take the risk, and the pair seemed to be rubbing along well enough together. One toasting, the other buttering. And the dragon eating . . .

The moon – back to its workaday silver tonight – was rising above the brick pit like a shiny sixpence. It had waned by a sliver from the full moon of the night before – that Blood Moon whose red glow had filled Tom with foreboding, and which had brought Tiddy Doll's death in its wake.

But Stick knew nothing of all that as he climbed the steep path up and out of the pit, and set off towards the thick pine-woods that encircled Darkling Hall and the village.

The smell of resin reached into his nostrils, clawing more memories out of the cupboard at the back of his head. *Pine trees kill anything that tries to grow beneath them.* That's what someone had said to him once, a long time ago. And she'd added, 'If I could, I would tear them up and plant a hundred cherry trees in their place.'

In the moonlight, drooping grey branches sheathed the pine trees like shrouds. Stick shuddered. *I still hate them mirksy things*, he thought.

He hesitated. Stopped at the edge of the trees. He wasn't sure he could do this.

Looking up at those towering shapes framed against the moonlit sky, he was a child again, seeing one-legged giants with branches for arms, stretching down to snatch him up.

Ahead, under the branches, there was no light at all. The pines swallowed the moonlight into their own darkness. He knew he'd be able to see nothing once he stepped beneath that thick canopy. He would have to follow his memory of the path that led to Darkling Hall, after years of trying to forget.

Still Stick hesitated. He knew he had to do this, he had to find Spud and Sparrow before they ended up in the pit with his unreliable new friend the dragon. And he had to stop Sir

202

Jasper before he gave up on digging the dragon out and simply blew up the pit.

But it was so dark under those trees.

'Fly . . .' He found himself saying his old friend's name out loud. He'd never needed her so badly. Fly, who'd hated the rats that crept amongst the gutterlings at night and tickled their toes as they slept on the streets, but who'd never let her fear show, because she knew that Stick hated the darkness even more. So she'd take his mind off it by shying rocks at the rats and laying bets with him to see who could hit the biggest one. *Coo, weren't them rats just something!* He could hear her now.

And then, in that moment, Stick believed he really could hear her. 'Wotcher, my cully!' Her voice was so clear he looked round, expecting to see those dark eyes flashing under a mop of black hair, and that dark, heart-shaped face grinning back at him. She wasn't there, of course. But he felt as though she was, even though she'd left him and sailed away to another land, a thousand miles distant and more.

'Chin up, my cully!' Fly was saying. 'Spot of dark can't hurt you!' He'd never told her why he was scared of the dark, never told her what had happened to him. And she'd never asked. But she'd always been there when he needed her. And he felt her so strongly now it was like she was here.

'We'll be out the other side of them shummocky trees in two shakes of a lamb's tail,' she promised him.

The first step was the hardest, even though he was feeling less alone. 'It's all rug, Stick. Just keep going. I'm here,' Fly was saying. The second and third steps came easier, and then he was walking, putting one foot in front of the other, trying not to look back as the blackness and the thick, suffocating smell of resin closed in around him.

The only sounds now were his bare feet on the deep bed of pine needles. Their softness tricked him into trusting them at first, until a sharp up-ended point jabbed savagely into his sole. 'Drabbit it!' He hopped over to lean on a tree trunk whilst he pulled it free, but he nearly lost his balance and the rough bark scraped his skin raw beneath Scrope's shirt.

'I know you don't want me here, any more than I wants to be here,' he told the trees.

A breeze stirred the branches and the pine trees whispered back, *'You are not welcome here. Go back to the gutter.'* They were standing guard like they were Sir Jasper's army, tasked with keeping Stick from returning to Darkling Hall.

As he crept forward – more cautious this time about where he put his feet – the darkness grew denser. He had to put his hands out in front of him to stop himself walking slap-bang into the trunks. He warded off the low branches that clutched at him, but now and then a higher branch tapped him on the shoulder, and he'd leap as if he'd been caught prigging a hankersniff by the crushers.

'Blimey, Fly!' he whispered. 'I'm as jumpy as a box of frogs!'

But he had no doubt he was heading the right way. Some dark force was pulling him, drawing him towards the place he dreaded, the last place on earth he wanted to go.

He'd been stumbling onwards for what seemed like hours, but could have been only minutes, when his eyes caught a pale glimmer ahead. He thought at first that he had made it out the other side, or that it was a break in the trees, maybe a glade where the moon had managed to break through the gloom.

But then it turned out that darkness was not the worst thing he had to fear that night.

In front of him, rising from the ground like the restless spirits of the dead, were shapes spun from silvery light, which writhed and twisted between the trees.

In Stick's eyes, they took on the shape of small children, ghosts with empty eyes and gaping mouths. At the same time came an unearthly weeping and wailing, like the shrieks of unquiet souls.

Were they the ghosts of the children the dragon had eaten? Were these their lost souls wandering the woods, calling for their mothers, unable to find peace?

'Fly!' cried Stick, clutching about him with his hands, as if he thought he might find her standing there beside him. But there was no reply. He'd never felt so alone.

His deepest fear, so deep he couldn't name it, was that the ghosts of Spud and Sparrow were rising up to reproach him for not saving them. Even though he no longer believed his dragon had eaten them, he had no idea what might have happened to them, in the hands of Sir Jasper. His dread was that he had come too late.

The shapes were drifting towards him, wailing as they came. Stick stumbled backwards, tried to run, but tripped over a fallen tree that was lying in wait for him. He fell into a cage of dry branches and watched helplessly, sobbing, as the spirits drew closer.

And then, as fast as they had appeared, the shapes were gone, sinking into the earth from which they'd risen. The wailing stopped and darkness and silence returned to the woods.

Stick sat up. He was still shaking. 'Blimey, Fly,' he whispered, in the hope she might still be there. 'What the dickens was that?'

'It be whatever you think it be,' came a voice from behind him. It wasn't Fly's sharp gutterling talk. It was the soft burr of a joskin, the country drawl he remembered from these parts. 'Had you in a right puckaterry, di'n't he, snotty-nose?'

Stick swivelled round, wiping his nose quickly on his shirt-sleeve. Standing behind him, casually swinging a little lamp, was a small girl he reckoned at no more than eight years old.

But this was no ghost. This was a solid, sturdy, country-cream-and-butter-fed child with thick, ginger ringlets that glinted gold in the lamplight. And she was grinning down at him in a way that very much put him in mind of Fly. A solitary green and white gingham ribbon was clinging amongst the curls. It was a perfect match for the one Stick still had in his pocket, but this didn't seem like the moment to discuss ribbons.

'What do you mean?' Stick demanded. For some reason this girl was making him feel like a fool.

'Them things you were seeing—'

'Ghosts . . . ghosts of children . . .' Stick's voice was still shaking.

The small girl sniggered, and Stick's face felt suddenly very warm. 'If you say so. 'Course, that be what he wants

207

you to see. He be wanting you to see whatever you're most frit of.'

'I ain't frit!' Stick tried to make it come out steady, but there was still a wobble. 'I know what I saw! And who's *he*, any road?'

'Sir Jasper, of course. Who else would be wanting to frit folk out of the few wits they've got? Who else would be wanting to scurrify everyone away from these woods . . .?'

'But how . . .?' Stick was still sure he'd seen what he'd seen, though he didn't take much persuading that Sir Jasper was behind it.

''Tis a phanta . . . phantabla . . . phantama-thingummyjig . . .' The word was too big for her.

'A phantasmagoria!' Stick helped her to the word, pleased to know something she didn't. He had heard of such things, at fairgrounds. They were the latest fashion, tricks of light and sound, which showmen used to make people see stuff they swore blind were ghosts.

'Mebbe. Any road, it be just a bit of codology, what makes lummuxes like you see things what ain't really there.' She tossed her ringlets smugly. She still knew more than him. 'Sir Jasper has been fritting everyone out of the woods with it, so they don't go near his blessed brick pit. They all thinks the woods is ghostified.'

'You mean, he wants to keep them away from whatever it is *under* the brick pit?' If Stick had guessed right about who this little madam was, she must know what was in the brick pit. She must be the one who had dared to tell off the dragon.

'Yeah, that wrinkly old bit of shoe-leather down there,' she said, casually. 'It were going to eat us all, after Sir Jasper threw us into the pit. It had already snaffled three of the kinchen, by the time I got down there. I give it a right mobbing, a real piece of my mind, I did.'

'She told me,' said Stick.

Now it was her turn to look flummoxed, much to Stick's satisfaction. Her mouth hung open like a herring.

'What d'you mean, she told you?' she demanded, reluctantly.

'Can't you speak dragon?' he jeered. It was his turn to be smug again.

Her green eyes widened until they looked like they might pop, and he smirked to himself. *That's shut her clack-box!*

'You're bamming! What – you twig what that thing is saying? You can *talk* to it?'

Stick shrugged. He wasn't going to tell this hoity-toity little madam everything. He'd already said a lot more than he was used to saying. Anyway, it was his thing. His thing and the dragon's.

209

He changed the subject, smartish. 'So how did you end up in the woods?'

'Well, that thing down there – arter I'd given it what for, and told it that there be no way I were going to let it eat me, nor my cullies, any time soon – it went bambling off in a huff down this tunnel. So the rest of us, we just climbed back up, through that little hole. Sir Jasper was gone, but when we got back to our village, it be all burned down . . .'

Her voice was wobbling. But she carried on.

'And they was all gone, Ma and Pa and my brother Tom – the whole village was empty. So I brung everyone back here, all the childers what had been yaffled by Sir Jasper and that bean-pole of a sister of his . . .'

'So there's more of you?' Stick said quickly. Maybe he wouldn't have to go up to Darkling Hall after all. Maybe Spud and Stick had ended up safe in the woods with this bossy little madam, somehow.

''Course there is – there's the childers from the village, what were yaffled same time as me. And a few joulterheads what they codded into coming from London – gave them a load of balderdash about three meals a day and . . .'

'And plum duff for afters?' finished Stick.

'Mebbe.' She frowned.

She don't like it when I knows more than her, observed Stick to himself with a secret grin.

'Any road,' she said quickly, before he could get another word in. 'What are you doing gammicking about in the woods, for that matter?'

'I'm trying to find my friends, Spud and Sparrow – you seen them?'

She shook her curls. 'There be none by that name out here in the woods. They probably be still locked up in that place . . .'

'Darkling Hall?'

She nodded.

'Whereabouts?' Stick was dreading the answer.

'In this real dark place, under the house. Right gloomy place it is, with a big stone tomb with no name on it.'

Stick had gone very pale. 'The crypt,' he said. 'I know that place.'

And he knew whose body lay inside that tomb.

CHAPTER 24

'Who's this then, Marm?'

Stick swung his head round. A circle of glimmering lamps had gathered behind them, like a cloud of glow-worms hovering under the branches. They up-lit the grinning faces of a score of children, all looking as game for a lark as Fly and the rest of the gutterlings had ever been. He recognised a few of them from the London streets.

They looks right as rain, thought Stick. *They don't look like being fodder for a dragon has done them much harm.*

'It's another lummox what fell for His Nibs's bit of jiggery-pokery,' Marm said airily. 'He stopped snivelling when I told him it was a load of bumby.'

'I weren't snivelling!' Stick bit back, but then he stopped. However irked he was by this little drabble, he really didn't

212

have time to argue. He still had to get up to Darkling Hall before it got light, to rescue Spud and Sparrow.

'Any road, I'm off.' He got to his feet.

'Without us?' Marm looked indignant. 'You'll never find your way up there on your tod.'

'I knows my way.'

'What'll you do when you get there? Knock on the door and ask them to let you in?' she sneered.

'There's another way into the crypt,' Stick said shortly.

'Gammon and spinach!' For the first time since she'd twigged that Stick spoke dragon, Marm looked impressed. 'We was locked up down there for ages and we never found no way out. You're codding!'

'No, I ain't,' replied Stick. He wasn't going to explain. Wasn't going to talk about the last time he had needed to escape from that place. He dusted off the pine needles that were sticking out of his kecks like the prickles on a hedgepig. He was ready to go.

Marm was silent for a moment. But she clearly didn't want to miss out on a lark. 'And what you going to do then? With a load of kinchen and nowhere to hide them?' she demanded. 'You needs me to come with you!'

'And me!'

'And me!'

There was a chorus of eager voices. Nobody wanted to be left out, if there was an adventure to be had.

Stick considered. 'Come on, then. But you ain't coming in with me. You can wait on the edge of the wood. And you'll have to stash them glims when we get close. Don't want Sir Jasper and his sister looking out the windy and seeing a load of lamps fossicking about in the dark.'

He set off, and they followed, quiet as mice. It seemed like they'd taught themselves to move soundlessly through the woods. Truth be told, however annoying Marm was, it felt a lot more companionable to have her little army sniggling through the trees behind him, instead of being alone with nobody but an imaginary friend.

It was still pitch black under the canopy. But above them, up in the tree-tops, the heavy silence of the night was lifting. The earliest birds were stirring and twittering to one another, with their usual cheerful optimism that a new day was dawning and would bring good things with it. *I ain't so sure about that*, Stick thought.

'We needs to mizzle,' he whispered to Marm, ''Tis almost day-glim.' He increased his pace. He would have to cross the open lawn surrounding the house to find the secret doorway. An open lawn that could be watched over from dozens of windows.

Dang me, I hopes it's still there. It hadn't occurred to him until now that the hidden opening – known only to him and one other – might have been discovered in the years since he'd been gone. It had been their secret. *You must remember this, if I am gone, and you need to get away . . .* she'd told him.

He understood now. She'd known she was dying. She'd known he would need a way out, after she was gone. It had been her way of protecting him. But perhaps Sir Jasper had found it and closed it up, after he had escaped?

The trees were thinning at last, and ahead Stick could see the expanse of lawn, thick with cobwebs that had been silvered by a dawn drench of dew. Still dark enough if he hurried. He gestured behind him, and hissed, 'Put out them glims!' Then he crept cautiously to the edge of the pine-wood.

Darkling Hall loomed solid and black ahead. Joined to it on the right-hand side was a turreted tower, the last remaining part of a much older building. Its golden stone shone like a candle beside the grim building. *A good deed in a naughty world* – that's how she'd described it.

He realised he had started hearing that long-lost voice again, after years of trying to forget – that voice that he hadn't been able to let himself hear since he'd fled this place so many years ago. He still couldn't remember her face, but now, for the first time, he found himself wanting to remember.

The tower was all that was left of the fine castle that had stood here for centuries. But it was many years since this place had been home to any knights.

The ugly brick building called Darkling Hall had been built by Sir Jasper after he had torn down the castle. He'd ordered black bricks made specially to his taste. It was square and dark and uncompromising, overlaid with thick ivy and neglect. A fortress, glowering down on the village in the valley below.

Rows of windows like blank eyes stared out at Stick. *'Turn around. Be gone. This is not your home,'* they were saying.

Stick had taken a vow that he would never come back, as he'd lain hidden in that rattling cart-load of sheep, bound for London. And now here he was, and his flesh was creeping at the thought of the evil lurking behind those forbidding walls.

'Where is it, then?' Marm crept up beside him, her green eyes shining with excitement. 'This secret place?' She squeezed his hand. He looked down at her small fingers, weaving themselves between his, and for the first time he felt more comforted than irritated by Marm's presence.

'Over there, at the bottom of the tower. My fam—' He stopped himself. Still not ready to tell too much. 'Someone built a hidden staircase, up from the crypt that comes out there, mebbe in case they ever needed to scarper in a hurry. In case their enemies got in.'

The trouble now was that the enemy was already inside. And the worst thing was, they'd been invited in.

Marm's little band was gathering around them. 'What now?' one of the boys asked eagerly. They didn't seem to feel any fear. Not like Stick. But they didn't know everything he knew.

'You lot stay here,' Stick said. 'We can't all go fossicking about – them two will hear us, and we'll all end up locked up, or worse.'

This time they did have the sense to look nervous.

'When I've got the others out, I'll send them back here, and you can hide them from Sir Jasper in the woods.'

Marm had heard something in his voice. 'What about you?'

'I needs to do something else after I've got them out, afore I comes back.'

Marm looked like she might argue, until she saw Stick's face.

'I'll come and find you, in the woods, when I'm done,' he said firmly.

She nodded.

'But if I don't come back . . .' Because he'd always known he had to plan for that. 'If I don't come back, you needs to go down to the pit and rescue that poor old cove what I've

217

left down there with the dragon – before that guzzle-guts thinks about eating him. Promise?'

Marm nodded, and he had no doubt she would do it.

'And . . .'

'What?'

'You have to get the dragon out, somehow, afore Sir Jasper blows her to kingdom come.'

Marm looked doubtful about that bit.

'I know she ate them kinchen,' added Stick. 'But she's really sorry about that now. And she don't deserve to get snabbled by that evil varmint.'

Marm nodded then, green eyes solemn.

Stick knew it was a lot to ask of a four-foot-nothing chit of a thing, and he couldn't rightly see how she was going to do it, but he'd learned that sometimes you had to trust people. And without Fly here, he reckoned Marm might be the next best bet.

But now he couldn't put it off any longer. It was time to face his demons.

Stick didn't bother looking up again at the accusing windows. If those two monsters were watching, he was kippered anyway. He took a deep breath and darted across the wide lawn towards the tower. He barely felt the cold, wet cobwebs sucking at his bare feet, trying to slow him down. He just ran for the safety of the golden tower.

He paused, breathing hard, when he got there, and looked back. Marm's raggle-taggle army had melted into the woods. He couldn't see them but he knew they were in there, watching and waiting for him and it made his heart beat warmer.

But then he noticed the tell-tale trail of dark footprints he had left behind him in the silver dew. Nobody came up to Darkling Hall without an invitation. Sir Jasper would know he had an intruder as soon as he looked out of the window.

'Drabbit it!' Stick swore. His footprints would be pointing like an arrow towards the secret opening, until the sun got up and burned off the dew. He had to be quick.

The foot of the tower was surrounded by bushes, which had got thicker since he had been there before. It all looked very different to him now from the way it had looked to a six-year-old boy. But he knew the entrance was somewhere round the back, near where the tower wall joined the main house. He crept round, parting the bushes here and there, trying to see in. At last when he guessed he was in the right place, he lay down and started burrowing on his belly under the branches.

Once he got to the wall, he stood up behind the bushes, and stroked his fingertips over the surface of the stone, as she'd once shown him. *There's a shape like a shield . . . it's hidden in the wall . . .* Long, slim fingers helping a child's chubby fingers to find the place. *There, can you feel it? It is the family crest . . .*

'Found it!' breathed Stick in answer, just as he had then.

He pressed the shield, and the block of golden stone shifted and slid back, smooth as a hot knife through butter. 'They made it well all those years ago,' she'd said. 'They made it to keep us safe in our hour of need.'

Stick stepped through the gap and into the tower. In the dim light he could see a narrow, circular stone staircase that wound both up and down. One way went up to the top of the tower. One way went down to the crypt. It was cunningly built into the thick walls so nobody would ever know it was there. He felt with his fingers for the shield he knew would also be on the inside of the wall. He hesitated.

Should he close the opening? Once he pressed it the stone would slide back in, and he would be in darkness. Cold fingers squeezed his guts. The place he most dreaded lay at the foot of those stairs.

'Pize take it,' he muttered. 'I wish my dragon were here. Wouldn't need no glim then.' But it wasn't just a dragon's fire that Stick was in need of. A dragon's heart was what he needed most of all.

221

The cupboard at the back of Stick's head was wide open now, and the horrors he'd kept in there were tumbling out so thick and fast he could hardly think straight. But remembering his dragon made him feel stronger, like she was breathing fire into his heart.

Spud and Sparrow is just down there, he reminded himself. *Nobbut a pig's whisper away – any minute now they'll be rabbiting on about why it took me so long to find them!*

So he pressed the shield and the stone slid back into place. He was in complete darkness and it smelled dank and cold as death.

Stick forced his feet down the winding steps, hands braced against the damp stone on each side to stop himself falling headlong. Down and down he went, until he sensed – before he felt it – the solid wall at the bottom where the foundations of the tower met the outside wall of the ancient crypt. Sir Jasper had knocked down the old chapel above ground, but he'd left the underground crypt beneath his new house.

Stick ran his fingers over the stone, trying to still his panic when he couldn't immediately find the shield. He stopped and took a breath.

'Drabbit it, I know for certain sure it's here.' He got the stem of his broken pipe out of his pocket and chewed on it

222

to calm himself. 'Don't get all of a fluster,' he told himself. 'Try lower down. You was smaller, then.'

This time it worked. Just as it had at the top, the block of stone slid away, and he stepped back into the crypt that he had escaped from all those years before, and visited in his nightmares ever since.

CHAPTER 25

It was the soft sobs Stick heard first, and that cold fist gripped his guts again. His mind was overwhelmed by memories now he was back here – they were coming at him so thick and fast he couldn't tell what was real.

'Is it you?' he whispered. And then, 'Don't be a fool,' he scolded himself fiercely. 'She's dead.'

Stick bit down hard on his bit of pipe. *It ain't Spud or Sparrow*, he thought. *I ain't never heard them blubbering.*

No matter how cold and hungry they'd all been on those long winter nights when no toff would stop and pay to watch them, and their dib-dabs were too frozen to do handsprings, it was a matter of pride that no tumbler would ever cry.

But he'd come here to find them, so he called their names out anyway. 'Spud? Sparrow?'

Stick's voice echoed round the stone crypt. He was shivering.

Last time he'd been here, he'd been just six years old. That long, lonely night, locked up in the darkness, alone but for her dead body. Clinging to her hand, as she lay on the cold tombstone. Not being able to bring himself to leave her, even though she'd reminded him what he must do to escape before she'd closed her eyes for the last time.

This was the memory that had woken him, sobbing, every night of his life since then.

'That's never Stick, is it?'

Stick's heart flapped like a flounder's tail. It sounded like Tree, but that couldn't be right.

There came the sound of a Lucifer striking and a candle glimmered on the other side of the crypt.

'Blimey, Squinty! You got another candle squirrelled away? Why didn't you say?'

Was that Bandy? Another flap of the flounder's tail in Stick's heart.

'You never asked,' said another voice, indignantly.

That was definitely Squinty, thought Stick.

'Cabbage-for-brains.' An impatient sigh that sounded just like Tree again.

225

What the bejeepers is they all doing here? thought Stick. Surely his mind was playing tricks on him again. Last time he'd seen the gutterlings, they'd been safely snoozling on Pickled Herring Stairs. That seemed like a hundred years ago. How had they all ended up here? And where were Spud and Sparrow?

But then two shapes came cartenwheeling towards him out of the shadows, and Spud and Sparrow were punching him and hugging him like they didn't know whether they were more angry or overjoyed to see him.

'Where you been 'til now, mutton-head?'

'Thought you was never coming for us!'

'Thought as you'd forgotten your old friends!'

'What kept you, addle-pate? We been locked up down here for weeks!'

'It ain't been weeks!' protested Stick, though he had to agree it felt like it. 'Got here as fast as I could, didn't I?' He was having to defend himself from their punches. 'Had a little matter of a dragon to deal with on the way.'

'Dragon! My eye!' retorted Spud, but Stick let it go. Time enough to tell them everything when they were all safely back on Pickled Herring Stairs, telling tales of an evening. If they did all get back. Which seemed far from certain.

'How did you get in here?' It was the horse-yob from the country, Tom, who Stick remembered hanging about on the steps back in London. *What's he doing here?* Stick wondered.

'There's another way in,' said Stick shortly. 'And out.'

'How did you know?' demanded Cess. He wondered why her face was all wet. They were all crowded round Stick now, and he was starting to get twitched. He'd never liked an audience, and he didn't even know half the faces that were staring at him now, looking for answers.

'I was here afore, long time ago,' he replied.

'Told you,' Tom said smugly. 'Said I had seen him in that trot-box, togged up in his velvet pantaloons.'

Stick glared at him. 'Who is this joskin, any road?'

'It's Turnip Tom,' replied Cess, but Tree gave her a shove.

'It's just Tom,' Tree snapped at her, before Tom could say anything. 'And we'd never have found Spud and Sparrow and the rest of them without him.'

'But mebbe we'd never have ended up in this hell-hole!' Bandy challenged Tree.

'And Tiddy Doll would still be alive!' Cess snapped back at her sister.

'That's not Tom's fault,' hissed Tree.

Cess shrugged and turned her back on Tree. 'Changed your tune about Turnip-boy, ain't you?'

Stick stared. He'd never heard Tree and Cess arguing before, but there was more important stuff to wonder about.

'What's happened to Tiddy?' he demanded. He'd known all along that it would be dangerous coming back here. But he'd thought the danger was all for him.

'We got snabbled, soon as we got to my village,' replied Tom. 'Sir Jasper and that sister of his—'

'Gertrude.' Stick nodded.

'They sent their men and they knocked us all on the bonce, and when we woke up, we was down here . . .'

'Except Tiddy didn't wake up.' Cess sounded broken.

So it was Cess who had been sobbing when he'd arrived. She'd always been the one who looked out for Tiddy. *Like a mother to her, she was*, Stick thought.

'Where is she?' Stick spoke softly, to hold down the fury.

Cess led Stick over to the still bundle at the foot of the stone steps. He looked down at the small body. They'd closed her violet-blue eyes, and she looked like she was sleeping.

'Them devils will pay for this,' Stick vowed fiercely. The anger burned hot in his throat. Another body lying dead in

228

this dank crypt. Another life they had taken. 'That pair is wicked, through and through, and I is going to stop them.' He turned back to the others. 'Come on. We needs to get out of here.' The other street urchins and the village children had been hanging back in respect for his grief, but now they stood ready to follow his lead.

Stick gently gathered up Tiddy's body, and carried her towards the narrow opening at the back of the crypt. She was no weight in his arms. The others followed him.

As he passed the tomb, its walls blank of any name, Stick whispered fiercely, 'I'll be back. And I promise you won't never be forgotten no more.'

Tree went first through the doorway, and the gutterlings followed her up the stairs, one by one.

'Wait for me half-way up,' Stick told them.

But they had left it too late. There was the sound of a key grinding in the lock, and the heavy oak door swung open at the top of the stairs, down at the other end of the crypt.

Stick looked back. Gertrude's skinny frame was silhouetted in the light that flooded in. She was wearing a white nightdress, grey hair loose and wild as a buzzard's nest, and she screeched like a banshee when she saw the gutterlings disappearing. 'Brother! Hurry! The little vermin are escaping!'

'Out of my way, you fool!' Sir Jasper's barrel of a body appeared, thrusting her to one side. She missed her footing and tumbled, shrieking, down the stone steps.

Tearing a voluminous nightcap, reminiscent of a cream puff, from his head, Sir Jasper strode in his nightshirt down the steps towards the gutterlings, stepping over his sister at the bottom. He didn't pause to pick her up. He just kept coming, the nightshirt flapping around his hairy knees.

The gutterlings were all through at last, and only Stick and Cess were left.

'Quick, Cess, take her!' Stick thrust Tiddy's body into her arms. 'Follow the others – up the steps! I have to close this door behind us.'

When she was safely through, he slipped after her, fumbling for the shield inside the stairwell. He pressed it hard.

The stone began to slide smoothly shut, but it was agonisingly slow. It was still not fully closed when Sir Jasper's beetroot head leered in through the opening. Stick saw his bloodshot eyes widen in recognition.

'You?' he bellowed, but then he had to pull his head back before the thick stone crushed his skull like an egg-shell.

Stick pushed his way up between the gutterlings who had gathered in the dark on the winding staircase. Half-way

230

up, where Tree was waiting, he stopped at the secret doorway to feel for the shield on the wall.

Again, the stone slid smoothly away. The early morning light flooded in, and with it the sweet smell of a new morning.

'Go quickly – he won't be long after us!' he said to Tree. 'Run across the lawn – there's a little madam with ginger curls—'

'Marm?' cried Tom, who was standing next to Tree. 'She's my sister! She's safe?'

'She's safe, right enough,' replied Stick. He could see Marm's curls flaming like a beacon as she waved at them from under the trees. 'She's got some sort of gang she's bossing about in the woods – she'll look after you all.'

Bandy took Tiddy's body from Cess, and they all ran towards the woods, all but Sparrow and Spud. They didn't budge.

'What about you?' demanded Sparrow. The tumblers were finally together again, and they weren't going anywhere without Stick.

'We ain't leaving you,' Spud chipped in, just to make it clear.

Stick hesistated. There was nothing he wanted more than to go back to how things used to be. To be back on the

231

streets throwing handsprings, with Spud and Sparrow beside him. The old life. But that was gone.

'You can't come with me.'

'Don't be a nick-ninny!' protested Spud. 'We ain't going nowhere without you!'

Sparrow was indignant. 'You can't have larks without us!'

But even as he said it, they all knew this was no lark. Even Spud and Sparrow had seen enough of the horrors of this place to know that.

'I has to do this on my own,' Stick insisted. 'Any road, I needs you to do something, and I don't trust no one else to do it.' He felt bad, using flummery on his friends, but it did the trick. The tumblers' eyes lit up.

'I needs you to go and rescue my dragon.'

Spud snorted. 'There ain't really no dragon . . .' But he stopped when he saw Stick's face.

'If I don't—' Stick paused. 'If I gets held up, you needs to get Marm to show you the way. And when you finds the dragon, say that her knight sent you.'

There was a wobble in his throat, but he swallowed it.

'The dragon will understand what you say, but you might not twig what she's saying to you.' He still wasn't sure why he was the only one who seemed to talk dragon but there was no time to think about that now.

232

He finished, 'Tell her I said to give Sir Jasper and his sister a proper scorching, so they can't hurt anyone else.'

And with that, Stick turned his back and carried on up the winding stairs, towards the top of the tower.

He was alone again.

CHAPTER 26

'She was a lily-livered little fool!'

At the sound of that bellowing voice, Stick swung round to face Sir Jasper.

'Father,' he said, and the bile rose in his throat with the naming of him.

Sir Jasper had thrown on some clothes before hunting Stick down. He'd found Stick standing in the centre of the little turret room at the top of the tower, staring, transfixed, at the picture on the wall.

Stick made no attempt to run away. It was this picture he had come to see. He had known all along he couldn't leave Darkling Hall without seeing her, no matter the risk. It was the portrait of a dark-haired woman with eyes as light and grey as drops of sea-water, whose face Stick had never let himself remember until this moment. His mother.

'She wasn't a fool,' Stick replied. He wasn't scared now. He was just very, very angry. 'She was brave, and kind, and good. And you killed her, you and that sister of yours. You broke her heart and you crushed the spirit out of her until she couldn't bear to live any longer. Not even for me. Not even for her son.'

Fly and Spud and Sparrow would not have recognised Stick at this moment. The skinny gutterling, who never said nowt unless he had a plan, stood tall, squaring up to the man he'd feared all his life. And for once, he had no idea what he was going to do next.

'You shut me up in that crypt with her dead body. A six-year-old boy. Your own son. You left me to die.'

Sir Jasper just smiled and turned to consider the portrait, as if it was the first time he had looked at it. 'She was pretty enough, I suppose,' he said carelessly. 'But her looks didn't last.'

'You kept her shut up indoors until she faded away. Hedged in by those pine-woods that she hated. You hardly let us out.' Even their trips to the village, when Stick had gone with her to watch her healing the sick – even that had been stopped by Sir Jasper, towards the end.

'Your mother couldn't be trusted.' It was Gertrude, who had entered the turret room, unnoticed until now. 'She would have run off, like the flighty little thing that she was.'

She'd hobbled up to the tower in pursuit of her brother, after changing into a stiff black bombazine dress. She looked like a badly sharpened pencil, topped by wild grey hair that was escaping from a hastily made bun.

'Auntie.' Stick nodded at her. There was such a flame of anger burning in his heart that if he could have opened his mouth and roared dragon-fire, he would have turned this pair to ashes in an instant.

He hated them even being in this room. It had been his mother's sanctuary, the place where she'd held Stick up to look out of the window every evening to say goodnight to the world. Although they could never see past the dark pine-wood. *I used to be able to see all the way to the fields, when I was a child, before he planted those trees*, she'd told Stick. The sweet, green fields where she went to gather her herbs. They'd been looking out of this window when he'd asked her whether the red glow from the brickworks beyond the trees was Hell.

He turned to his father. 'Why did you marry her, if you didn't love her?'

236

Sir Jasper laughed. 'I wanted her family name. Your family name, though you will never own it now!' His laugh wasn't a pleasant sound. It was the sort of laugh that would make babies cry and dogs whimper.

'Brave-Coeur,' he went on. 'That's your family name – it goes back to William the Conqueror, you know, and I took a fancy for it. Once she was dead, I took her name for myself.'

He said it with the same greed that he had for everything – from a prehistoric dragon to the heart of a long-dead saint.

'I became a knight,' his father boasted. '"Arise, Sir Jasper du Brave-Coeur!" – that's what that fool of a king said.' A snort of contempt. 'And then those peasants in the village had to bow and scrape to me.'

'You will never be a true knight,' Stick told him. What was it the dragon had said? *A true knight is pure of heart* – that was it.

But Sir Jasper ignored him. 'And, of course, I wanted to get my hands on that clay-pit which her fool of a father never had the sense to turn into bricks. I have made a fortune out of that mud!' That laugh again.

'Why did my grandfather make her marry you?' Stick barely remembered the weak little man who had crept about the house until he'd done Sir Jasper the favour of dying and leaving his daughter and grandson to his mercy. Why had he invited this evil man into his house and given away his only daughter to him?

'For my money, boy. Have you learned nothing down there in the gutter? Money is the only thing that matters. Money and meat. Which reminds me . . .' Sir Jasper rubbed his hands together, red as raw beefsteaks. 'In addition to all the other trouble you have caused me today, you are delaying my breakfast . . . Devilled kidneys, I think?' He raised a black, bushy eyebrow at his sister.

Gertrude was hovering, hanging on her brother's every word. 'And liver, dear brother. Bloody and rare, just as you like it,' she added eagerly. 'The calf was slaughtered fresh this morning.'

Gambling on his father being distracted by the anticipation of all that offal, Stick darted for the door to the secret stairwell which he had left open, in case he needed to get away. He'd got half-way through, his foot on the top step, when a great ham of a hand grabbed his arm, twisting it behind his back like a twig, until Stick thought it must snap.

'Let me go, you devil!' But he couldn't get free.

'So this is your family's secret stairwell?' Sir Jasper peered past him to look down the spiral steps.

Stick said nothing, biting his lip against the pain. *Not so secret now*, he was thinking. *But I don't reckon I'll be in need of it again, any road. My chances of getting out of here alive ain't worth a bean.*

'I suppose that's how you got out of the crypt, after we had tucked you up down there with your dead mother?' Sir Jasper didn't wait for an answer. 'We did wonder – but to be frank, we didn't much care, did we, Gertrude?'

Gertrude nodded. 'Good riddance, that's what we thought, brother, good riddance to the little brat.' She had a way of dipping her head and gazing up at her brother sideways when he paid her any attention, like a love-struck worm.

'Well, one way or another, we will make sure to dispose of you for good, this time.' Sir Jasper smacked his lips as he looked at Stick and for a moment Stick thought he might be considering adding his son to the list of creatures he'd boasted of eating. 'But first – breakfast!'

If the servants were surprised to find a grubby and decidedly smelly gutterling tied to a chair at the breakfast table, most of them were too cowed with fear to say anything. The only one who paid him any attention was an elderly footman, who stared at him like he'd seen a ghost. They all wore the same faded green livery, so frayed and moth-eaten that Stick reckoned they were the same togs as the servants had worn when his mother was alive.

They ain't going to be any help when it comes to a plan, Stick thought. He wriggled his fingers, but they were too tightly tied to reach his broken pipe stem, still tucked into the pocket of his kecks.

Stick watched as the servants brought in more and more dishes laden with offal, which Sir Jasper emptied as fast as they brought them. *Reckon as that's the innards of a whole cow gone,* Stick thought. After spending half his life wondering where his next meal was coming from, he'd never felt less hungry.

'Shall I lay a plate for your . . . for the boy, my lord?' It was the elderly footman who'd been staring at Stick. He got a clip round the ear in reply, which sent him staggering back on his unsteady old legs.

'Don't be a fool. Why waste good food? He won't be around long enough to digest it.'

Gertrude nibbled on a water biscuit, watching anxiously lest her brother's plate was left empty for a moment. He had tucked a capacious white napkin over his red waistcoat. By the time he sat back, as a signal he was finished, it was stained red and brown from blood and gravy.

He pulled it off with a sigh and wiped bits of gristle and grease from his glistening chin and bristling moustache.

'Excellent. Now – what to do with this sewer-rat?'

'Perhaps . . .' Gertrude began, her eyes fixed on her brother's face.

'Perhaps what? Spit it out, woman!'

'Perhaps it might be the case that we discovered this dangerous ruffian after he broke into the house while we slept . . .' she said slowly, watching for signs of approval.

Sir Jasper nodded, so she carried on. 'We have, of course, never seen the creature before . . .'

'Don't know him from Adam!' Sir Jasper joined in, encouragingly.

'And we found him stealing that precious portrait, the only image you have of your dearly beloved, sadly departed wife. So what could we do, but tie him up . . .'

'And shoot him?' Sir Jasper suggested, with a grin of delight.

Gertrude coughed, delicately, into her hankersniff. 'I was thinking more that we should put him in the hands of justice, brother. And let justice have the bother of disposing of him.'

241

Sir Jasper frowned. 'Shame not to shoot him, though.' Then his face brightened, and he hauled himself to his feet. 'But no, you're right. Messy and unreliable. Might miss. I'll send the carriage round for the magistrate, my old friend Sir Ralph.'

'Do invite him for lunch, brother! And tell him there's no need to go to the bother and expense of a court case,' Gertrude called after him. 'We can sort it out quietly between us, here at Darkling Hall, and the brat will be on his way to Australia by nightfall.'

'Australia? Fiddlesticks!' Stick heard Sir Jasper snort, as he strode across the hall to bark an order for the carriage. 'We'll have him taken to London and strung up at Newgate in the morning! Don't want any chances on him coming back and claiming his inheritance!'

CHAPTER 27

It was over a very fine lunch a few hours later that Stick was sentenced to death by hanging. Not that he got to eat any of it. He was still tied to the hard chair, his bottom had gone to sleep and he had pins and needles in his feet. *But I reckon that won't seem so bad when I is standing on the gallows at Newgate, come morning*, he thought.

He'd watched Sir Jasper and Sir Ralph guzzling what seemed like a whole henhouse of chickens, washed down with four bottles of fine claret. He still hadn't felt hungry. His father's table manners were a great quietener of the appetite.

Even beneath his wine-flushed cheeks, Sir Ralph looked a little pale at the sight of his host stuffing half a chicken into his mouth at one go, bones and all. Gertrude nibbled quietly on another water biscuit, but her sharp eyes missed nothing.

So it was she who pointed out, when Sir Ralph finally cleared his throat, in preparation for passing the sentence of death (after Sir Jasper had finished passing around the port) that the magistrate had forgotten to don his black cap.

'Forgive me, sir, but after all, we would never want it said that justice had not been done, and this matter had not been dealt with by the book.'

'Quite right, quite right, my dear lady,' Sir Ralph blustered. 'I have my black cap in my carriage. When I heard of the outrage that had been committed by this hardened criminal – you could have been murdered in your beds! – I naturally assumed it would be needed. My man will get it for me.'

So the hardened criminal sat patiently as the black cap was sent for. It arrived, and was settled by Sir Ralph's footman, like a dead bat, on top of the magistrate's grey wig.

'Before I pass sentence on you for the act of breaking into the home of a knight of the realm and stealing the one remaining image of his much-mourned wife, is there anything the prisoner has to say?'

'Gadzooks, man!' Sir Jasper exploded. 'Surely we don't need to hear anything from this blackguard . . .'

Sir Ralph looked alarmed, 'Quite right, quite right!'

'As it happens, I do have something to say,' Stick interrupted. He hadn't said a word since he'd been dragged in and tied to the chair, and now everyone, including the servants, turned to stare at him.

He went on quickly, before Sir Jasper could bully the beak into shutting him up. 'I ain't no crib-cracker. I is an honest tumbler by trade . . .'

Here he paused and considered the truth of that, but there was no call to admit to a little pickpocketing at this moment. And the burglaries had really been very few and far between – only when he and the tumblers had been really starvacious. So he continued without mentioning all that.

'. . . and I came to Darkling Hall from London to find my friends, who'd been snabbled off the streets and brought here by Sir Jasper and his sister. They codded them into coming here by promising them an eddication and three meals a day, with plum duff for afters.'

'My dear man, you cannot continue to let this guttersnipe spout such nonsense,' spluttered Sir Jasper. 'Why would we—'

But Stick hadn't finished. 'And then they took some of them childers, and threw them down into the brick pit, to feed the dragon what's living down there.'

A guffaw of laughter rang round the table. Even the servants were sniggering. But not the elderly footman, Stick noticed.

'What arrant nonsense!' barked Sir Jasper. 'Really, Sir Ralph, we do not need to listen to these ravings.'

Gertrude joined in, 'The boy is clearly touched in the head, quite mad. And dangerous! I am quite faint with terror!'

'Any road,' Stick could see that Sir Jasper and his sister would try to sufflicate him with their bare hands if he tried to say much more. 'The last thing I wants to say afore you shuts me up and sends me to the gallows, is this . . . That man over there is my father. I ran away from this place when I was six years old, after my mother died – after that wicked pair killed her – and he has stolen my name and my rightful inheritance—'

At this, Sir Jasper got to his feet, his chair crashing to the floor behind him. 'Great snakes, sir, are you going to allow this . . . this sewer-rat to blacken my good name and to speak of my poor dead wife in this way? Is this gutter-creeper to be allowed to cause me such pain? The cruelty of impersonating my poor dead son, who pined away after his mother died, and lies buried next to her in the crypt below our very feet!'

246

Gertrude joined in, mopping her face with her hankersniff. 'How can you allow this filthy scum to tell such lies about my brother? Really, sir, I fear for my brother's mind, to be reminded of his grief by this imposter!'

Sir Ralph stood up too now. 'This is an outrage!' he declared.

For one mad moment Stick thought the magistrate had believed him, but then Sir Ralph went on. 'Not only to break into this house, to attempt to steal Sir Jasper's most precious possession, but now to tell such terrible lies! If I could hang you twice over, you black-hearted villain, I would do so.'

He paused and adjusted the dead bat, which had slipped over his face in all the excitement. 'I sentence you – what's your name?'

'Stick, sir.'

Sir Ralph raised an eyebrow. 'Stick,' he said, like he had a bad taste in his mouth. 'I sentence you, Stick, of no fixed abode – I presume you have no fixed abode?'

'Nobbut Pickled Herring Stairs at present, your worship.'

The magistrate sighed and started again, 'I sentence you, Stick, of Pickled Herring Stairs, to be taken from this place and hanged by the neck until you are dead. And may God have mercy on your wicked soul.'

'Not sure as God will care much,' replied Stick. 'He ain't taken much note of me so far.'

'Wicked, wicked!' clucked Gertrude, like an egg-bound hen.

Sir Jasper was rubbing his red hands in glee. 'Excellent. Do you have time for a cigar, Sir Ralph?'

On a nod from Sir Ralph, Stick was untied from the chair and dragged out into the hall. He had a brief glimpse of the suits of armour, ranged round the hall, which he remembered from his childhood. Tarnished and dull now, from lack of care. *They were brave knights who wore that armour*, his mother had told him. Each of them held a long lance in its metal gauntlet.

My old scorcher would love them suits of armour, Stick thought fondly. *Take her right back, it would.* He hoped the dragon hadn't run out of crumpets yet. He'd never thought he'd miss her, but he did. And he could have really done with her help right now.

Stick's legs were as wobbly as junket, and Sir Ralph's men had to carry him out to the cart, which had been waiting for some hours to carry the prisoner off to Newgate. There had never been a chance of any other verdict. Guilty until proved guilty.

The men had finished chaining him by the ankles and were mounting the front of the cart, when the old footman who had been staring at Stick so hard crept out of the house.

'Here, my lord,' he whispered. 'I brought you some vittles.' He thrust a small pork pie into Stick's hands. 'I knows who you are, my lord – I believes you, every word you said.' His voice was shaking. 'You looks just like your dear mother. She was the sweetest woman what ever lived, and she loved you more than life itself.' He stopped. There were tears running down his cheeks, which were as wrinkled as an apple that had been left out too long in the sun.

Stick recognised him now. It was this man who had given him piggyback rides round the hall, when he was a small boy playing at being a knight. One time, Stick had insisted on trying to carry one of those long lances, but he couldn't even lift it, and he'd sat on the hall floor and cried until the footman had picked the lance up and helped him to hold it.

'Simkins,' he whispered. Another memory slipped out, a memory which explained something that had always puzzled him. It was Simkins who had bundled him into that cart full of sheep and safety, all those years ago. That was how he had got away, after he'd crept out of the crypt and up the secret staircase, leaving his mother's body behind him. Simkins had found him at the foot of the tower, blinking and tear-stained.

'It was you,' Stick whispered, and Simkins nodded.

'Out of the way, you old fool!' one of the coachmen shouted.

Stick leaned over the side of the cart, as far as the chains would allow and Simkins caught hold of his hand. 'Will you go to the woods for me? Tell Marm – she's the little bossy one with the red hair . . .' The old servant smiled, like he knew who Marm was. *I reckon everyone round here knows who Marm is*, Stick thought.

'Tell her that Sir Jasper will be on his way to blow the dragon to smithereens, now he has no kinchen left to feed to her as bait. So Marm has to get her out of the pit, smartish!'

There was a crack of the whip, and Stick felt the cart jerk as the horses started forward. He clung to the old footman's hand. 'And Spud and Sparrow – they're my . . . my friends . . .' His voice got stuck on something. 'Tell them, every time they chuck a cartenwheel, to put a penny in the pot for their old friend Stick . . .'

That reminded him of something, and he felt in the pockets of his kecks with his other hand. There were three pennies and a couple of farthings left of the money the tumblers had made at Bartlemy Fair. It seemed so long ago now.

250

'And can you give them these? It ain't much but it won't be no use to me where I'm going. And say I is sorry, but I bought a saveloy and some saloop without them being there to share.'

Their hands slipped apart. 'God bless you, my lord!' the old man shouted after him. 'And my lord – your name ain't Stick – your mother called you . . .'

But the name his mother had given him – which Stick had long kept locked away – was lost in the rattle of the wheels and the cloud of dust kicked up by the horses' hooves, as the cart set off to take him to Newgate and the gallows.

CHAPTER 28

Marm's country joskins and Tree and Cess's band of gutterlings were still eyeing each other suspiciously over bowls of hot rabbit stew, when they heard the rumbling of barrels of dynamite down towards the pit. It was their first inkling of what Sir Jasper was planning next.

The newly escaped gutterlings had been gobsmacked when they clapped eyes on the pot bubbling over the fire at Marm's camp in the woods. They didn't entirely trust food that hadn't been prigged off a stall. But the city urchins who had escaped from the pit with Marm reassured them.

'It's all rug, Tree,' one of them said. 'We been eating this stuff for weeks and none of us has croaked yet.'

The crossing-sweepers, Squinty and Bandy, were

already on their third bowls, but Cess had hardly touched hers. She was sitting apart from her sister, next to the small, still body of Tiddy Doll.

Tree was poking at her second bowl, keeping a close eye on Marm, who was a sight too pushy for her liking. Marm had gone to sit on the far side of the fire from her brother, Tom, who hadn't been able to stop hugging her. 'Leave off, Tom! Stop mithering me!'

But Spud and Sparrow had left after their first bowl and were prowling round the edge of the camp, on the lookout for Stick. So it was them who came rushing back to tell the others about the barrels.

'It's that cove with the beetroot face!' panted Spud.

'Old raspberry – he's got all his men rolling these big barrels between the trees,' Sparrow chipped in.

'And we don't reckon they is full of oysters, 'cos they've got a skull and crossbones painted in red on the sides,' finished Spud.

'Like for "danger"?' guessed Bandy.

'I had a bad oyster once what should have had "danger" painted on the side,' Squinty chipped in. 'Near killed me, it did.'

'Shut your clack-box, Squinty,' Tree said sharply. 'What's that varmint up to now?'

253

'I knows what he's doing!' said Marm, with a smirk at Tree. 'Stick told me that Sir Jasper was planning to blow up the dragon, and I had to stop him.'

'What dragon?' demanded Tree, bewildered. She and Cess had heard nothing about any dragon until now, and they didn't like being the last to know about anything.

'Stick told us about the dragon too.' Spud backed Marm up, and Tree looked daggers at him. 'We thought he were bamming, at first. But then he told us we had to go with Marm and give the dragon a message.'

'But we weren't to do nowt unless Stick didn't come back,' insisted Sparrow.

'He ain't coming back, though, is he?' Spud replied miserably. 'He'd be here by now, if he was coming back. Something's happened to him.'

There was a silence. Then Marm stood up. 'Well, we'd best get a hustle on, ain't we? We has got a dragon to save. And there's some old cove down there with him too, hiding from Sir Jasper. They is both going to get blown up, once His Nibs gets his barrels down there.'

'But what's happened to Stick?' Cess lifted her head from watching over Tiddy. She didn't give two beans for some mythical creature nobody had even bothered to tell her about.

'My lord is on his way to Newgate, to be hanged on the

gallows.' It was the quavering voice of the footman, Simkins. The old man looked as though he had run all the way from Darkling Hall. 'He sent me with a message,' he panted.

His knees buckled under him, and Tom caught him before he collapsed to the ground.

'Get him some water, Marm.' Tom was the only one who dared boss Marm around.

'What do you mean, he's on his way to Newgate?' The tumblers couldn't bear to wait for an answer.

Marm kneeled down beside Simkins and gave him his water. He opened his eyes. 'Is that Marm?' he asked. She nodded.

'My lord said—'

'What's this "lord" business?' interrupted Sparrow. 'Does he mean Stick?'

'I told you I saw him wearing velvet pantaloons,' insisted Tom. Spud and Sparrow stared at him in disbelief. They hadn't heard that bit of the story.

'Yes – the boy you call Stick – he is the rightful heir to Darkling Hall,' Simkins said faintly.

'This old cove must be loose in the attic!' declared Spud. 'Stick ain't no toff.'

'Give him some more water,' said Tree anxiously. 'He's looking a bit pale about the gills.'

They gave Simkins more water, but they were all impatient to get the rest of the story now. They could hear the ominous rumbling of more barrels going down to the pit.

'My lord – Stick – sent me. He said to tell Marm to rescue the dragon before Sir Jasper blows up the pit.'

'I told you so!' said Marm, triumphantly.

'I'll give you a larruping you'll never forget, if you say that again,' growled Cess. She was no keener on Marm than her sister was.

'But did he not say anything about us? And what has they nabbed him for?' asked Sparrow. 'Why is he being sent to Newgate?' He could hardly get the questions out fast enough.

'Are you Spud?'

Sparrow shook his head and pointed.

'Sparrow, then? My lord gave me this for you both.' The old man was fading. He patted the pockets of his servant's livery, and pulled out three pennies and a couple of farthings. 'He said to think of him every time you turn a cartenwheel.' He gasped for air. 'And to give you your earnings, because he would have no need of them now. He said he was sorry, but he'd spent some of it on saloop and a saveloy.' Another gasp, that might have been a sob.

256

'Here, let him rest,' said Tom, laying Simkins down gently on a blanket someone had found. He turned to the others. 'Sir Jasper must have snabbled Stick after we left, and codded the beak into sending him to Newgate on some trumped-up charge.'

'He'll be hanged!' Spud wailed. Stick would never have believed it, but both his fellow tumblers were blubbering now.

'Well, we ain't going to let them do it!' Sparrow dashed the wet stuff from his face.

'What can we do, though?' Bandy and Squinty had faces as long as fiddles. 'Nobody never comes out of Newgate, except on the end of a rope.'

'Yes, but nobody normally don't have no dragon!' retorted Marm, standing up. 'Stick said I should tell her to give Sir Jasper and his sister a good scorching. But I reckon that before we do that, we should get the dragon to spring Stick from Newgate.' They all sat staring at her. Nobody moved.

'Come on!' she snapped. She tossed her red curls, losing her remaining green gingham ribbon in the process. 'It's no good sitting there like a load of dying ducks in a thunderstorm! Get up and do something!'

It took a while to get everyone ready, with Tom insisting on making Simkins comfortable before they left. Marm was hopping around like a box of frogs, and Spud and Sparrow gave up waiting and set off down the path to the pit.

'We have to go, Cess,' said Tree quietly to her sister.

Cess was still fussing over Tiddy Doll's small body, checking she was safely tucked up in blankets. 'She hates being cold.'

'That old cove Simkins promised me they'll bury her proper,' Tree said, holding out her hand. 'And one day we'll come back and see her . . . but we can't stay here now.'

So at last Cess stood up and took her sister's hand, and together they followed the others out of the camp.

When the gutterlings reached the edge of the pit and peered down, it was clear they didn't have much time. There were forty barrels in there already, and Sir Jasper was bellowing at his men. 'Get a move on, you lazy loblollies!' He turned to one of them. 'No sign of that fool, Scrope?' he asked.

'No, my lord. The cottage is empty, and the bed's not been slept in. Looks like he's skedaddled.'

'Well, I can't hang about waiting for him. It's time I made some money out of that beast down there.' He bellowed again, 'One more trip! Then I'll blow this place sky-high and get my hands on those bones at last!'

258

He followed his men back towards Darkling Hall, to collect the last load of barrels and the fuses to light the dynamite.

'We needs to be quick,' said Marm, elbowing her way past Tree and Cess to the edge of the pit. She pointed. 'That's the place he threw us down. Come on.'

'I swear I'll have that little chit's guts for garters when this is all over,' hissed Tree under her breath, but both she and Cess had to admit that they couldn't find the dragon, nor save Stick, without her, so they followed in silence.

'Blimey!' swore Spud, as they squeezed through the hole in the bottom of the pit and slid and slipped and slithered down the slope. 'Stick owes us a snossidge or two arter this.'

'SNOSSIDGE!' came an eager cry from below, and they saw two huge yellow eyes gazing up at them, attached to a creature the size of a London omnibus.

All the gutterlings heard was a roar so hot it singed their frayed kecks. But there was no time to go back now, not with the barrels of dynamite about to be blown up above their heads. So, one by one, Marm's gang and the gutterlings bumped to the bottom.

A snout as big as a cart sniffed at each of them in turn, but when it came to Marm, she put her hands on her hips defiantly. 'You ain't sniffing me, you old buzzard. I know your game – and you ain't eating any of us, neither!'

'I don't eat children any more,' the dragon insisted, but all everyone heard was more roaring. Although they could tell she looked a little hurt.

The dragon swung her snout to a dusty little man who had crept from the shadows of the cave. 'Tell them that I don't eat children,' she said again, but all Scrope heard was roaring, too.

'Oh, you useless creature!' The dragon sighed. 'Where's a knight when you need one?'

Scrope looked terrified. It had clearly been a nervous night for him, once the crumpets ran out.

Spud nudged Sparrow. 'Remember what Stick said – she can understand us, even if we can only hear a load of roaring. Tell her . . .'

'You tell her, you're bigger than me!' retorted Sparrow. It was the first time Spud had ever heard Sparrow admit he was the smallest.

Spud took a deep breath. 'Here goes.' He pushed forward to stand next to Marm.

'Well, madam,' he started, because Stick had told them to be sure to be polite. 'It's like this, milady. Beg pardon, but Stick told us to say that your true knight had

260

sent us, and that you had to give Sir Jasper a good scorching.'

The dragon nodded, so they could see she understood. She snorted back, 'Well, where is he, then, if he's my true knight? Which seems extremely unlikely, given that he has grown up in a gutter.'

Marm butted in impatiently. She wasn't going to bother with buttering up the old buzzard. 'Thing is, you shifty old scorcher, we needs to get a mizzle on, 'cos Stick has been yaffled by Sir Jasper and he's been sent to be strung up at Newgate. And the least you can do, to make up for gobbling down them three cullies of mine, is to help us to save him.'

'Newgate? That is indeed a terrible place. I have many times heard the poor prisoners groaning in their cells, as I passed underneath. Hanged, you say? What a barbarous race you humans are!' They heard her give a loud sniff. 'I have to admit I had grown fond of that little chap. And he did make my poor paw better – look – good as new!'

The dragon tried to stand on three legs to show off her nicely healed foot, and almost overbalanced. The gutterlings scattered quickly to avoid getting crushed. She sniffed again.

Sparrow nudged Spud. 'Look, I swear she's getting wet around the winkers.'

'Never mind all that! Tell her that we're all about to get blown up!' Tree snapped. They could all hear Sir Jasper bellowing with excitement from the edge of the pit. He had returned with the last of the barrels and was getting ready to light the fuse.

'I'm getting to that!' Marm snapped back. She turned back to the dragon. But the beast was already waddling away down the tunnel.

'Come along, you lazy calf-lollies!' she called back. 'Look lively! We need to get to Newgate. There is not a moment to lose.'

Nobody had a clue what she was saying. But they didn't waste any time in following her.

They were quickly joined by Scrope, his dusty whiskers twitching as he scurried after them. 'Goodness me, I am not accustomed to palaeontology being quite so eventful!'

It wasn't a moment too soon. Sir Jasper had already lit the fuse, and a tiny blue flame was snaking towards the towering pile of barrels.

'Stand back, Gertrude!' he called, rubbing his red hands together in eager anticipation of the slaughter to come. He had brought her with him to witness his triumph over the dragon.

'You don't think you might perhaps have overdone the dynamite, brother?' asked Gertrude, and there was more

262

than a touch of anxiety in her voice. It was the first time she had ever come close to questioning her brother's authority. And, as it turned out, it was the last.

'Nonsense, woman!' But Sir Jasper's shout of joy was lost in the colossal explosion that swallowed up the brick pit. And the edge of the brick pit on which he and his sister were standing. And the brickworks. And the pine-woods that lay between the pit and Darkling Hall.

There was nothing left of Sir Jasper, nor Gertrude. Not even enough to fill a sausage.

Sir Jasper's men very sensibly had already run away, so they were half-way home by then, and well out of harm's way. And the dragon and the band of joskins and gutterlings had got far enough along a few bends in the tunnel to escape the full force of the blast.

The brick dust from the explosion stained the sunset an angry orange, and long into the night, the blaze of the burning resin in the pine trees lit the sky with the same blood red as the moon, just two nights before.

CHAPTER 29

Stick was lying on the cold stone floor of a Newgate cell when he felt a low rumble, like thunder, but coming from beneath the ground. It took him back to the day this had all started at Smithfield, when the blood had melted between the cobbles, and his heart skipped a beat for a moment.

He sat up. *Mebbe it's the old queen, come to get me.*

But then nothing happened, and Stick recalled how dark the skies had been when the cart bringing him from Darkling Hall had rumbled into London. The Great Heat had been threatening to break at last, and lightning was already crackling in the air. But still there had been no rain to wash away the sins of the long, hot summer.

It's just thunder, he told himself, and he lay back down, trying to share out the pain between bits of his body that were already bruised from lying on the bare stones. But he couldn't move much, because the prisoners were packed into his cell as tight as ticks.

Any road, the old scorcher will be long gone by now, he thought. *Stick and Spud will have got her out of that pit, somehow.* And he tried to screw his face into smiling as he imagined his dragon soaring into the skies, free at last. He'd never seen her fly, and he suddenly wished with all his soul that he could have seen that sight, before he died on the gallows in the morning.

He hugged his knees to his chest for comfort, wanting to believe that the dragon was free. He told himself, quietly, 'That little madam, Marm, she's sharp as a box of monkeys, considering she's just a joskin. Besides, there's Tree and Cess and the rest of them – the gutterlings always come up with a plan.'

But you're the one what's dabs at making plans, Stick, he heard them saying to him, and truth be told he didn't really hold out much hope that his dragon wasn't already dead, and Sir Jasper wasn't at this very moment boiling the flesh from her bones.

Stick shuddered, and it wasn't just the cold of the floor. He was remembering Sir Jasper's boast about getting a taste of the dragon's heart. 'You devil!' he swore out loud, and got a clout from his neighbour for disturbing his sleep.

It was the longest night of Stick's short life, a night of endless bitter hours lying awake and cursing his father, broken by brief blissful snatches of sleep, full of dreams of his mother's face.

He was dreaming of his mother when a prison screw, with a face as mean as a meat-hook, shook him awake and offered him a final meal of fish-porridge or a dry crust.

'I ain't hungry, if it's all the same to you, mister,' Stick replied, but from the clout he got over the ear in reply, it seemed that not eating wasn't an option and was regarded as the height of ingratitude, so he gnawed on the dry crust until the screw went away.

It was dawn, but it was still as dark as midnight when they led Stick up from the cells and shoved him out on to the wooden walkway to the gallows. An uneasy crowd stirred in the prison yard below, but there was none of the usual holiday atmosphere. Nobody looked at Stick. They were all watching the black clouds that were blotting out the sun. Even the street-sellers' cries of 'Hot pies, hot as they come!' were subdued.

Everyone was waiting for something to happen. But nothing fell from the threatening skies, nothing but the odd raindrop, each as fat and heavy as a plum. It was as if the clouds had forgotten how to rain, after weeks of relentless heat.

The preacher that Stick remembered from Bartlemy Fair

266

was pushing his way through the crowd. 'Repent, for the Day of Judgement is upon you, and the Devil will drag you down to Hell!' he was shouting. And from the mood of the crowd, they seemed inclined to believe him this time.

'They say there's a flood coming,' was the murmur that was going about.

'Old Scratch has been roasting us in our beds long enough – now we're all to be drowndead.'

'Like in the Bible it is, forty days of drought . . . next news it'll be a flood. Where's Noah when you need him?'

'What then? Plague of frogs?'

But even the Old Testament couldn't have predicted what was to come. Because it turned out that the rain was the least of their worries.

As Stick was shoved towards the waiting gallows, a rumble grew below the cobbles of the prison yard. Shrieks went up from the crowd, as the earth groaned and bucked and rippled, like a snake shuffling off its skin. Men and women alike went down like ninepins. It felt like the rumpus at Bartlemy Fair, all over again.

'Lawksamussy!'

''Tis the end of time!'

At the same moment as this earthquake appeared to be taking place beneath their feet, the heavens opened and

267

sheets of rain lashed down. It felt like the Thames had burst its banks above their heads. The Great Heat was ending.

But the crowd were too comfoozled and comflobstigated by what was happening beneath their feet to worry about the deluge that was falling on their heads. The rumble under the earth kept growing until it turned into a roar, and the cobbles began popping out like cannonballs. The screw who'd been pushing Stick on to the gallows platform took a direct hit on the head, and collapsed into the chaos of the crowd below.

'Blimey!' cried Stick, looking down into the chasm that was opening in the prison yard. 'It's the old queen, come to rescue me!'

Stick had never seen his dragon in her full glory before. Her gold-crowned head rose up through that sea of fools who thought it was fun to watch a child die on the gallows. She reared up out of the earth and stretched to her full magnificence, her head as high as the grey stone walls of Newgate.

Gone was the dusty yellow of fading autumn grass. Her shining scales were the deep glistening green of fresh holly leaves in the spring. And she spread her crimson-edged wings, which he had never seen unfurled, and beat them with all the joy of her freedom from the earth.

'What larks!' she cried, but it was only Stick who heard anything but roaring.

The first flap of her wings sent the gallows tumbling into the crowd, and Stick was left clinging to the wreckage of the wooden walkway.

'Come on! Jump, you booberkin!'

So Stick leaped for his dragon's back, landing between her wings and clinging on to the spikes of her corona. It was healed now, and shining as it had in her prime.

'I don't remember when I last had this much fun!' She tittered gleefully. 'Shall I scorch them? We could start a little fire, like I did before!' He could feel a rumble in her chest as she stoked up her flames.

Stick looked around at the ruckus of terrified Londoners, climbing over each other in their hurry to get away. He considered for a moment what was the right thing to do.

'I don't reckon they all deserve it, milady,' he said, slowly. 'And besides, the crushers will be on to us in two shakes, and they'll be taking pot-shots at you again with them muskets.'

'I suppose you have a point.' The dragon grunted in disappointment and he felt the rumble very reluctantly subsiding.

'Stick!' There was a cry below him. Emerging from the great gaping hole in Newgate's prison yard was a bedraggled gang of gutterlings and joskins, led by Spud and Sparrow. Scrope's battered black gown flapped out behind them.

'Up here!' Stick waved down at them. 'Climb up!' he shouted, forgetting for a moment that the old scorcher might not take kindly to a crowd of gutterlings scrambling up her sides. And then he remembered that she wasn't entirely reliable when it came to kinchen, even if she had saved his life.

'Not likely!' called back Spud. 'We ain't getting up there!'

Sparrow joined in. 'You must be loose in the basket if you think we're getting any closer to that thing!'

'We has had enough of this lark!' shouted Spud. 'Besides, my belly thinks my throat's been cut.'

'Come on, Stick,' added Sparrow, 'we can get us some decent prog, now we is home, 'stead of that maw-wallop what the joskins eat . . .'

Stick felt like he was being torn in half. Part of him longed to be chucking cartenwheels with the tumblers or back on Pickled Herring Stairs with a stolen fire-bucket, listening to the stories from the streets. Maybe after all that had happened, he'd even break his usual silence and tell his own story tonight . . .

But how could he leave his dragon? He looked down from his perch between those improbably small ears and felt all the joy of her new freedom pulsating beneath her scales. He even thought he could feel a heartbeat. It was like a drum-roll of deep happiness.

'Come back with me!' he begged the tumblers. *There would be room for everyone in that house*, he thought with a fierce yearning. It was his closest thing to family, down there.

But they shook their heads. 'Come with us,' Spud insisted. 'We've got enough dibs for three saveloys!'

He understood. He could see they were itching to get back to the streets, back to what they knew. It was a bigger hunger even than the hunger for saveloys. It was a hunger for what you called home.

It had been the same for him when Fly had begged them all to go with her and her tiger. He hadn't wanted to leave then, because he'd thought the gutter would always be his home. But this time he knew where home really was for him.

He'd spent years forgetting, but now he'd been forced to remember. And he knew there was stuff he had to do. He had to go back and repair the evil that had been done by his father. To earn back the name his mother had handed on to him. *Brave-Coeur*.

So in the end Stick shook his head too. 'I have to go back,' he shouted. It was one of the hardest things he'd ever said.

Tree and Cess heard what he said, and Cess called up,

'Take care of Tiddy Doll for me, Stick!' Her voice cracked. 'Bury her in a field somewhere with a naffy view of the sky. She loved them stars.'

Stick nodded. 'I promise. You can come and visit her, one day.' He saw Cess smile and nod and he knew that she, at least, would come.

Then there was nothing left to say. It was time to leave. *How do you gee up a dragon?* he wondered.

'Come on!' he whispered into one of those tiny ears. 'Time to go.'

'No last scorching?' she asked, ever hopeful.

'No, ma'am. Let's go.'

Stick saw a flash of red curls below, and thought he heard Marm shouting, 'Take me! I want a ride on the dragon!' but he shrugged and set his face for Darkling Hall. He had work to do, and she had to learn that she couldn't *always* have her own way. Marm and Tom and the other joskins could find their own way home.

A great flap of the dragon's leathery wings sent the last stones from Newgate's walls crumbling to the ground. The dark clouds parted and the sun greeted the dragon in her glory as she soared into the skies above the city.

CHAPTER 30

What with one thing and another, nobody had got round to warning Stick about the colossal hole in the ground where the brick pit used to be.

After all, there wasn't much opportunity for conversation with the dragon. It had been all he could do to hang on, as she merrily swooped and circled and did figures of eight in the sky, with the sheer joy of being free of the earth at last. But he had drawn the line when she tried to do a loop-the-loop and fly upside down.

'Get me the right way up, afore I lobs my groats on your corona!'

After that things had calmed a little, and Stick was able to look down on the patchwork of drought-baked yellow fields below. Sunlight glinted silver on the shining bends of the Thames behind them, like a great scaly tail coiled protectively round the city.

As they drew closer to Darkling Deeps, Stick felt around in the pocket of his kecks with his free hand. He needed his pipe, even if it was broken. He needed a plan for how to get rid of Sir Jasper and his aunt Gertrude. Would he have to kill his own father? But first he realised he owed the dragon a confession.

'I needs to tell you something, milady,' he yelled in her tiny ear.

'No need to shout, guttersnipe! Still no manners!'

'That man, Sir Jasper . . .'

She nodded, which wasn't the best idea with Stick perched on the top of her head. He clung on tighter, clenching his teeth grimly round his broken pipe. He'd never said this out loud before.

'You know you said I smelled like him?' It still made him sick to say it. She nodded again, but he was ready for it this time. 'Well, I never told you, but he's my father.'

He'd expected her to toss him off her head in disgust, but there was just another nod.

'*Was* your father,' she corrected him. 'I knew that, boy. But now he's dead anyway, so it doesn't matter.'

276

Stick gasped. It felt like when he'd fallen in that underground river, and all the dirt of the years had floated away down the stream.

'Sir Jasper – dead? But how?'

The dragon took a sudden dive towards the earth. 'That's how!' she crowed. 'Look!'

The place where the brick pit had been was now a red gaping hole, like a wound in the earth.

'Blew himself to smithereens with his silly little barrels,' the dragon told him. 'He thought he'd blow me up and boil my bones, but he was hoist with his own petard!'

Stick didn't have a clue what that meant, but it was clear nothing could have survived that explosion. 'What about Gertrude?'

The dragon shrugged, but then a tattered piece of black bombazine floated past Stick's head, and he guessed his aunt had gone with her brother to meet their Maker. Whoever that was. She, perhaps, had loved Sir Jasper in her own way, but his terrible all-consuming greed had destroyed them both.

Stick turned his gaze towards Darkling Hall, beyond the smouldering remains of the pine-woods. The house was his now. But he hated it. He promised himself he would pull it

277

down and rebuild it, in the same golden stone as the tower.

'Can you drop me off over there?' he asked the dragon, pointing to the house.

'Humph!' snorted the dragon. 'I am not a hackney cab for hire!' But she swooped down obligingly and landed on the lawn.

Stick slid down off her head, his arms following the curves of her scaly neck like a caress. He walked round and stood in front of her snout, feeling suddenly awkward.

What would the dragon want to do now? Would she just go off and find another cave somewhere? Or would she – heaven forbid – want to come and bunk up with him? She wouldn't make the easiest house guest, even in a house as big as Darkling Hall. But how to say goodbye? Something was making his eyes prickle.

He was about to ask her in for a cup of tea, hoping there might be crumpets, although he had no idea whether there were any servants left and whether they would obey the orders of a filthy little gutterling anyway. But then she spoke first.

'You are a true knight,' she said.

'What?' said Stick.

278

'Close your mouth, boy. When it hangs open like that it makes you look like a halibut. I said, you are a true knight. Even if you don't look like one.'

Stick closed his mouth and said nothing. What could he say? He didn't feel like a knight. But he didn't really know what he was any more.

She went on, 'As I was about to say, you have a debt to pay. I saved your life. Which is completely against any of the ancient rules of chivalry and dragon-slaying.'

Stick nodded, although he wasn't familiar with any of those rules. But he could see her point, leaving aside that by any fair reckoning, he'd saved her life first with that poultice.

'I think I mentioned to you, when we first met, when you failed to provide me with a snossidge . . .'

'Sorry.'

The dragon acknowledged his apology with a gracious nod but carried on. 'I mentioned to you then that I was weary of this life. It is a terrible and lonely thing, to be the last of your race . . .'

'You can stay here!' Stick had blurted out the rash offer before he'd really thought it through, but she brushed it aside.

'Very kind, dear boy. But you miss the point. You are my true knight, and I need you to—'

279

'No!' Stick burst out as he realised what she was about to ask.

This is where it had all been leading, since those first words to him, back there under Smithfield. 'I have lived too long . . .' she had said. 'That is the greatest tragedy in life – you cannot make your own heart stop beating.'

'No! I won't do it!' he vowed.

'You have to do it!' she snapped, yellow eyes flashing dangerously. 'Or, so help me, I really will eat you alive!'

And then she added, 'Please.' This time she really was pleading. Pleading for her death.

Stick was silent for a moment. He looked deep into her eyes, and he knew now for certain that it was a heart burning in there, not just flames. She had saved him from hanging. She had given him his life back. And now he had to do what she asked, and take her life away.

He knew what he had to do.

'I need to get togged up. I will see you at the top of the tower,' he said, as he turned and walked into Darkling Hall.

Inside the hall, Simkins the old footman was waiting for him.

'You'll be wanting your armour, my lord.' He'd been watching.

Stick nodded.

He'd never thought he'd grow to be big enough to fit into one of those suits, back when he'd ridden around that hall on Simkins's back, crying with frustration because he wasn't strong enough to carry a lance. But when Simkins buckled the armour over his tattered togs and the rags of Scrope's shirt, he realised how much he'd grown.

'Don't forget this, my lord.'

Simkins was holding out a lance. Stick took it and weighed it in his hands. He could do this.

The armour felt heavy, almost too heavy to walk in, as he took his first steps towards the door. But when he caught sight of himself in a long mirror, he believed for a moment that the dragon might be right. He looked like a knight. But was he?

Simkins called after him. 'There is something you should know, my lord. Your name isn't Stick. Your mother called you "George".'

Stick nodded. It had been the last thing left in the back of his cupboard. All the memories were out now.

When Stick reached the top of the tower, the sun was dipping in the west. The rain had revived all the sweet smells from the scorched fields around Darkling Hall.

I'll give this place a new name, he thought. *Something more cheerful.* Tiddy Doll would have liked that.

He looked out over the smouldering remains of the pine-woods. He and his mother had stood together at the top of this tower, but they had never been able to see this far.

'I'll dig out all those stumps and plant a hundred cherry trees, like you wanted,' he told her. 'And they will spell out your name in blossom in the spring.'

Amy. That had been her name. *It means 'Beloved',* she'd told him. He hadn't understood why she was weeping, then. 'I belove you, Mama,' he'd said.

He could see the charred cottages in the village below. Another reminder of Sir Jasper's wickedness. They'd need rebuilding.

'I'll send out word, and tell all the families it's safe to come back. And then Tom and Marm will have their Ma and Pa again, and all the kinchen can come home . . . Apart from three,' he remembered with a pang.

The church was still standing in the centre of the village. A quiet little graveyard sloped up the hillside next to it.

I'll bury Tiddy Doll there, he promised Cess, in his head. *Where she can look out over the fields.*

282

It hurt to think about the gutterlings he had left behind. But there was so much he had to put right here. Here, in the place he now remembered as his home.

The sun was glinting silver on Stick's armour, and his dragon saw it and swooped down from the sky towards him.

'My true knight!' she breathed, and she breathed her fire into his heart.

'Do it!' she commanded him.

He took a deep breath of courage. Then he lifted the heavy lance and threw it in a silver arc, as she flew high above his head.

He sobbed when he saw the point piercing the tender thrush-egg blue of her belly, and she gave a great cry of pain.

But then he heard her last words to him – 'Thank you!' – and she soared away, higher and higher, above the setting sun.

She flew on, her bright blood streaming down to the earth – on and on, until she reached the distant ribbon of the river, gold and crimson in the sunset.

The she turned and flew east, and he thought that brave heart would never stop beating. He followed her with every beat of his own heart, on and on, until the wide mouth of the river met the silver of the sea.

And then she plunged like a glittering arrow beneath the waves, and was gone.

AUTHOR'S NOTE ON STICK'S WORLD

This book started – as books so often do – with a walk. This particular walk – on a freezing January day with the promise of tea and cake at the end – lay through the ancient heart of London, and it followed in the footsteps of so many wanderers who have sought inspiration from the ghosts of Londoners past and the humour of Londoners present.

The walk began at the Monument, which marks the place where the Great Fire of London started in September 1666. And there she was – the City Dragon – waiting for me with her head peeping coyly out from the bottom of the fine carving around the stone plinth.

They call her the City's Guardian, and once you start looking there are dragons lurking everywhere around those streets. But there was an expression on this one's face that got me wondering about how that fire really started. Was it a burned loaf in Pudding Lane? Or a French spy? Or was it a mischievous old dragon lurking beneath the streets, who just wanted to shake things up a bit and watch London burn?

There was a look about that wicked little scorcher that made me smile then, and has kept me smiling through the writing of this book. I hope you love her as much as I do, even if she is a curmudgeonly and contrary old bird.

Those of you who have read *Tiger Heart*, the first of the gutterling books, will be familiar with Stick's world. It is a kind of time-slip between the wild rumpus of Georgian England and the brilliant inventiveness and energy of the Victorians. Like the gutterlings, I have prigged the plummiest bits out of this rich plum duff of a world, and fashioned a London to suit myself and to suit their story. And of course – unlike the gutterlings – I know that not everyone in the country has two heads and eats nowt but turnips. I happen to be very fond of the country.

Stick's gutterlings have a lot more larks than street urchins really did at that time. In reality, many orphans would have been doing horrible jobs for very little mint-sauce, and if they were lucky enough to have a bed, they curled up in it cold and hungry most nights.

King Billy in Buckanory Palace is not based on any real king, but he could be any king or queen who cared nothing about the starving children on their streets and kept their hankersniffs pressed close to their noses. In France around this time the people decided they'd had enough, and cut off the king and queen's heads to teach them a lesson. But that's another story . . .

STICK'S GUIDE TO GUTTERLING

(with a few bits of country joskin thrown in
for Turnip Tom and Marm)

A

Adam and Eve's – this was a pair of coves what liked to fossick about with no togs on. Don't know why the crushers didn't clap them in quod. But it means you is bare naked as the day you was born.

addle-pated – we has a whole barrow-load of names for fools what ain't got all their buttons on.

air-pie – if you has nowt to eat but air-pie you is going to be mighty starvacious. 'Cos there ain't nowt in it.

all (his) buttons on – when a cove is smart and dabs at coming up with larks and wheezes.

allicholy – miserable and full of the mulligrubs, with a face like a dying duck in a thunderstorm.

B

bags of mystery – just 'cos nobody knows what's in a sausage – or a snossidge – don't mean it don't taste good.

bambling – country joskins say this when they means shambling and wobbling about.

bamming – we says 'you is bamming' when we thinks someone is joking, or we can't believe a word they says.

beak – a magistrate, what would clap a gutterling in quod and throw away the key as soon as look at them.

Beelzebub – whether you believes in this old cove or not, there ain't no shortage of names for the Devil – like Old Nick, Old Bendy, and Old Scratch.

befuddled – a person is liable to get a bit confused and befuddled after a few too many glasses of gin.

bloaters – this is a kind of fish what's been smoked. Mebbe the safest way to eat them 'cos most of the fish on these streets ain't too fresh.

bobbery – any kind of ruckus and botheration.

bonce – this means head. Plenty of times a crusher gives you a smack on the bonce for nothing or less. Sometimes just for breathing.

booberkin – a cove what ain't got the sense they was born with.

bosky – same as tossicated – when a person ain't very steady on their feet after spending too long in the alehouse.

bow-wow mutton – the sort of meat you might get in your snossidge. Like as not it's not so much mutton as mutt.

bread-basket – this is the safest place to put your vittles – your belly.

brown bread – in London we likes to use words what sound the same as summat else, to confuse the country joskins and the furriners. If you is brown bread, you is dead.

bubbled – tricked or codded.

buffle-headed – same as addle-pated. No more wit than a coot.

bumby – one of them country splodgers' words for a load of rubbidge.

C

calf-lolly – this is same as a loblolly or a dunderhead. Not very smart.

carbuncle-face – a carbuncle is a kind of festering boil, so this ain't the sort of thing to call someone if you wants to butter them up.

chitterlings – if you has a rumpus in your chitterlings, it means you has the belly-ache.

clamjamfry – a right ruckus and noise and clomflobstigation.

Clare Market – no gutterling with all their buttons on would go to Clare Market. There's plenty of meat on the stalls, but there's no knowing what animal it come from. And them butcher-boys and costermongers is a bit too handy with a meat cleaver to make for pleasant company.

clod-pate – a nincompoop or a nick-ninny, with no more cunning than a dead pig.

cod – if you cods someone, you tricks them. There's plenty of codology and codocity on these streets, so a gutterling needs all their wits about them.

colly-molly – a cove what is allicholy and full of the dolefuls. But a gutterling ain't got time to mope about like a wet hen.

comflobstigation – confused and topsy-turvy. Usually 'cos a drink or two has been taken.

comfoozled – a cove what needs a little sit-down 'cos they is comflobstigated. Usually 'cos a drink or two has been taken.

coney – what them country joskins calls a rabbit.

costermongers – stall-holders what sell all sorts of stuff, but they is some of the most fratchety and bad-tempered coves in the whole of London, and no gutterling would be daffy enough to cross them.

cough-drop – a cough-drop is as nasty as poison.

cove – this is a word what you can use for any man.

crushers – we calls the police the crushers 'cos they'd crush our heads soon as look at us.

crying cupboard – if your belly is crying cupboard, it wants you to put food in it, sharpish.

cullies – your cullies is your friends, the ones you can trust.

cunning as a dead pig – not very cunning at all.

D

dabs – a dab is a little fish, no more than a few mouthfuls, so if you bet dabs to dumplings, to my mind you is better off taking the dumplings.

dabs at – my cullies always says that me and Fly is dabs at wheezes, 'cos we always comes up with the best plans.

daffy – a few pennies short of sixpence. Not very smart.

dib-dabs – don't get comfoozled with all these words like dibs and dabs. Dib-dabs ain't nothing to do with money or little fish – it's your fingers, or what we calls your fidgets. 'Cos they is dabs at dipping pockets and prigging stuff.

dibs – this is a word for money, like mint-sauce. Not that we ever has much of that.

dona – a dona is a woman. If it is some lady what's got loads of mint-sauce, we calls them a flash dona.

drabbit it – this is what you says when summat makes you fratchety and cross.

drabble – an irritating little tyke.

dunderhead – you can never have too many names for a fool.

dying duck in a thunderstorm – if you has a face like a dying duck in a thunderstorm, you ain't exactly going to be looking cheerful. The opposite of a gigglemug.

F

farthing – you can't buy much with a farthing – it's half of a ha'penny and not even enough for a hot potato. If someone tips us tumblers nobbut a farthing, Spud calls them a weaselly old skinflint. Which ain't too smart 'cos it don't make 'em inclined to give us any more.

fidgets – the same as dib-dabs or fingers.

flat – a fool.

flim-flam – when you is trying to cod some cove, best to make up a bit of flim-flam and humbug.

flounder – this is another one of them fish, but this one is flat and they says it lies at the bottom of the sea and goggles up at you with one eye. I reckon they ain't to be trusted, and mebbe that's why people sometimes says you is lying like a flat fish or a flounder.

flummergasted – same as comfoozled and comflobstigated – when someone is well and truly confused.

flummery – you needs to be dabs at flummery – wheedling and flattery and buttering up the toffs – to survive as a gutterling. And if that don't work, run away fast.

fossicking – if you goes fossicking about, you is just wandering around or mebbe searching for summat.

fratchety – curmudgeonly and bad-tempered.

G

gammicking – joskin-talk for when a cove is messing about and wasting time.

gammon – what you says when you reckon as someone is talking rubbidge.

gammon and spinach – same as what I just said, but even more rubbidge.

gander – when you gets a gander at summat, it means you takes a good look.

gigglemug – if someone is a gigglemug, they never stops smiling. Oftentimes that's 'cos they is addle-pated.

glim – a light, same as day-glim means dawn.

gummagy – when you is cantankerous and fratchety and not too happy.

gum-tickler – summat tasty what tickles your gums.

gutterlings – me and my cullies calls ourselves gutterlings 'cos most of us was born and bred in the gutter and ain't never known anywhere else. Other people has worse names for us.

H
half-inched – same as prigged or pinched – this is one of them sounds-like words.

half-seas over – there's plenty of coves on the streets what is half-seas over 'cos they has taken too many glasses of gin.

hang-gallows look – this is a word for mirksy coves what look like they'll end their days dancing from the gallows.

ha'penny – half a penny is twice a farthing, but it still ain't much of a tip for a tumbler. Mebbe enough to get you a stale bread roll.

havey-cavey – a good name for coves what ain't to be trusted.

hedge-fish – a varmint what you might find lurking about under a hedge and generally up to no good.

highty-tighty – on your high horse and a bit too pleased with yourself.

hopped the twig – same as brown bread. Dead.

horse-yob – a boy what hangs about offering to hold a toff's horse, in the hope of a tip. It ain't much of a job, to my mind.

house-breaker/house-cracker – same as a burglar. If you gets caught when you is house-cracking, it's the gallows or you is transported to 'Stralia, where they all walks upside down.

humbug – a load of rubbidge and codocity.

J
jabber – if a cove tells you to stow your jabber, they wants you to hold your hush or shut your chatter-box.

jiggumbobs – bits of jewellery and such-like.

jobberknoll – a fool. There is so many of them, you can't have enough ways to say it.

joskin – a cove what lives in the country, same as splodgers. They ain't half so smart as us gutterlings, an' we knows for a fact that most of them has two heads.

joulterhead – a joskin word for a jobberknoll. They got plenty of fools out in the country.

jumble-gut lane – most of them lanes out in the country is so rough that they rearranges your insides when you trots along in a cart.

junket – a pudding what's like jelly but made with milk. I ain't never tasted one, but I seen 'em wobbling around in shop windows.

K

kecks – sit-down-upons, or sit-upons. Trousers.

ken – if a joskin says he kens summat, he means that he knows it.

kicked the bucket – dead as a door-nail.

kinchen – same as childers: children.

kippered – smoked like a kipper. So you is dead.

L

lamming – if you gives a cove a lamming, it's going to hurt.

lamprey – if this ain't the ugliest fish, I don't know what is. Looks like an eel, but uglier. I heard tell it ain't bad in a pie though.

larruping – the same as a lamming. When a cove gives you a good thump.

less than a pig's whisper – if you do summat in less than a pig's whisper, it means you do it in no time at all. Mebbe pigs don't do much whispering.

lobbing up your groats – there ain't any nice way to say it . . . when you brings up your lunch.

loblolly – thick as a bowl of fish-porridge. Another word for a fool.

loose in the attic – someone who ain't got all their buttons on, a jobberknoll.

Lucifer match – matches what is a bit temperamental and liable to explode.

lummox – a loblolly what is clumsy as well as daffy.

M

maggot-brain – when a cove is so stupid it's like maggots ate everything inside their bonce.

maw-wallop – us gutterlings eats almost anything, but maw-wallop is prog what is so bad it has you lobbing up your groats soon as look at it.

mint-sauce – same as dibs. We has more words for money than any of us ever has pennies in our pockets.

mirksy – this is a word for a dodgy varmint or anything that looks dark and dirty and dangerous.

mizzle – when you has to scarper and skedaddle real fast.

mollocking – carrying on and causing a kerfuffle and a noise.

mopey as a wet hen – I ain't never had the acquaintance of too many hens, but I reckon they ain't happy when they has wet feathers.

mulligrubs – if you has the mulligrubs, you is allicholy and miserable. Same as a wet hen.

mussy – reckon this is just a muddled up way of saying 'mercy' – and 'lawksamussy' is what you says when you is real surprised or frit.

mutton-headed – about as smart as a sheep.

mux – if you makes a mux of summat, you has made a right mess of it.

N
naffy – summat what is really good.

nibblish hungry – us gutterlings is nibblish hungry most days but, truth be told, it would take more than a nibble to fill our bellies.

His Nibs – what we calls a toff or a swell.

nick-ninny – no more sense than a newborn baby.

noggin – another word for your bonce or your head.

nosh – food, or prog. Another thing we has plenty of words for, but not so much in our bellies.

numbskull – someone who ain't got much in the way of brains in their noggin.

O
Old Bendy, Old Nick, Old Scratch – all names for that old cove below-stairs, what they calls the Devil.

P
palaver – a botheration and a rumpus.

pandalorum – this is what Fly used to say when she was in a bit of a pickle.

parish pickaxe – if you has a nose like a parish pickaxe, it ain't exactly small. Or pretty.

penny-puzzlers – when you buys a sausage you pays your penny and then you can puzzle over what's inside it. But as long as it fills a hole, I don't rightly care.

pize take it – this is what you say when summat has made you fratchety and cross, same as 'drabbit it'.

plates o' meat – this is another of them things that sounds like summat else – it means your feet.

plum duff – plum pudding. Best if you can get 'em to give you the plummiest bits.

pother – if you gets in a bit of a pother it's the same as a botheration.

prig – every gutterling has to prig vittles some time, 'cos we'd be starvacious otherwise. Best just hope you don't get caught and locked up in quod.

prog – same as vittles and nosh. We ain't never got enough food.

puckaterry – this is what the joskins call it when you gets in a pother and a botheration.

Q
quod – prison. If the beak claps you in quod, you ain't likely to be coming out any time soon.

R
roosting-ken – somewhere to sleep.

rubbidge – a load of gammon or codswallop – rubbish.

rug – when your cullies say summat is all rug it means it's all right.

S

saloop – ain't sure what's they put in this. Some street-seller said it were orchid roots or summat, but I don't rightly know what an orchid is when it's at home. But it's a sight cheaper than tea or coffee.

saveloy – like a sausage but with even more pepper so nobody twigs that it's more than likely made out of horse.

scrobbled – kidnapped or half-inched.

sharp-set – if you is sharp-set, you is nibblish hungry.

shemozzle – any sort of ruckus or disturbance.

shotten herring – this is a herring what is well past its best and many days since it last saw the sea.

shravey – shifty, and not to be trusted. A havey-cavey type.

shummocky – a load of rubbidge.

skinflint – a cove what's mean when it comes to sharing his mint-sauce.

skinny as a rasher of wind – so thin you disappear if you turn sideways.

slubberdegullion – a filthy, slobbering varmint.

snabble – same as scrobble, 'cept sometimes worse 'cos you end up brown bread.

snaffle – can be the same as snabble and scrobble, 'cept sometimes it's when summat is gobbled down, 'specially when it comes to a dragon with crumpets and childers.

sniggling – creeping about and fossicking around.

snossidge – Spud reckons this is a better word than sausage 'cos it sounds like the noise you makes when you is snaffling them down.

snuff it – when you kicks the bucket and hops the twig and ends up brown bread.

splodgers – same as joskins. Splodgers live in the country, an' they eats nothing but turnips. So it's no surprise that most of them has two heads.

stand stall – all gutterlings knows how to keep watch for danger, soon as they can walk.

stick your spoon in the wall – another of them words for when you is dead.

stiff – a cove what's stuck his spoon in the wall.

swell – same as a toff. If us tumblers is lucky, they give us a tip. If not, Spud gives them a mouthful.

T

tarnal/tarnation – a word for summat really bad an' vexatious.

toff – same as a swell. Walks about with their nose in the air, an' crossing-sweepers has to clean the streets so they don't get their shiny boots and clean kecks dirty.

togs – this is what we calls clothes, but most of our togs is more hole than cloth.

tosher – a tosher is a sewer-hunter what fossicks about grubbing out coins an' such-like what's got washed down there. They ain't the sweetest-smelling coves.

tossicated – drunk. After a day at Bartlemy Fair and a few too many glasses of gin, there's a fair few who end up bosky and half-seas over.

totty-headed – another way of saying someone is a fool.

tow-row – what a gutterling shouts to warn that the crushers is on the way.

trot-box – a box what trots – a carriage.

trotter-boxes – don't get comfoozled – trotter-boxes is what you puts your trotters in, if you is a toff and can afford shoes.

tweak – if you is in a tweak, it's the same as if you is in a twitch, an' you need to take a good chew on your pipe an' keep calm.

V
varmint – a mirksy sort of villain what ain't to be trusted.

vittles – this is what we never has enough of in our bellies – same as prog or nosh.

W
wambling – the sort of feeling you gets in your belly afore you lobs your groats.

wet around the winkers – no self-respecting gutterling ever blubbers, no matter how cold or wet or starvacious they are. So you'll have to work this one out for yourself.

whey-faced – as white as a bucketful of milk.

woefuls – if you come over all colly-molly and you is wet around the winkers, that's the same as the woefuls.

Y

yaffled – this is what the joskins say when they means snabbled or snaffled. Don't know why they can't just talk King Billy's English, like us gutterlings.

ACKNOWLEDGEMENTS

I have a great debt of gratitude to my agent Lisa Babalis at Curtis Brown for laughing at my jokes (I think) and for her unfailing encouragement and wisdom. Also, to my editor Lena McCauley for making *The Dragon and Her Boy* the best it could possibly be, and for not batting an eyelid over the notion that there was a cantankerous old dragon lurking under Smithfield, less than a mile from her office.

A huge thank you to all the teams at Orion/Hachette who have worked so hard to make *The Dragon and Her Boy* such a beautiful book, including Alison Padley, Helen Hughes, Emily Thomas and James McParland. Also thank you to my copy-editor Emma Roberts and my proofreader Cat Phipps.

Stick's dragon owes so much to all those places in London where anyone can go and mentally fossick about in layers of time – most of it for free. From the dinosaurs who lurk in my nearby park at Crystal Palace, the fossils and finds at the Museum of London, to the street signs and ancient buildings of the City where you can walk the same streets as Stick and his gang of gutterlings.

I always want to say thank you to the Arvon Foundation, whose writing courses helped me to do what I have wanted to do since I was five years old – ever since I discovered that you could open a book and share the larks of a cast of characters whose only limits were the imagination of their creator.

Thank you to my children – Holly and Scott, and now Alexander and Sarah – for putting up with me and listening to me agonising about how I was ever going to rescue a dragon from a brick pit. The cake really helped.

And thank you to Barbara for accompanying me on so many of my fossickings, including that freezing day in January when we first spotted that wicked little scorcher at the bottom of the Monument.

And the biggest thank you, always, to Mum and Dad. No thank you will ever be enough.

Have you read *Tiger Heart*? Set in the same world as *The Dragon and her Boy*, *Tiger Heart* is a magical tale of a bold young chimney sweep, a remarkable tiger, a dangerously hypnotic ruby and a mystical land found across an ocean and through a storm.